Future Fiction

Edited by

Francesco Verso

Francesco Verso

Futurespotting

Published by Associazione Future Fiction
Via Valentiniano 40 – 00145 Roma
ID: 979620205888

Title: *Futurespotting*
© 2021 Future Fiction, Roma
I edition March 2021
info@futurefiction.org

Introduction

by Jana Vizmuller-Zocco

This collection of short stories by Francesco Verso illustrates his multifaceted and flourishing talent. He is the prototype of an indefatigable cultural entrepreneur: publishing world science fiction authors through his Future Fiction publishing house, writing prize-winning novels and short stories, organizing world science fiction conferences, enabling science fiction entry into the world of theatre, music, visual art, mass media and social media, to list only his most important activities.

A number of stories included here see the light after years of gestation or existence, others are brand new, some are extensions of situations contained in his novels (in particular, *Nexhuman* and *I camminatori*), and one was published elsewhere. Asimov's three scenarios are well represented by the stories offered here: "what if, if only, if this goes on"; however, these scenarios form not only the germ-ideas for the stories but also their consequences. The reader's engagement is doubly assured. The language is entertaining, full of neologisms, irony, puns (starting with the title), and tongue-in-cheek elements, impeccably rendered by the translators.

The stories fall into the category of speculative science fiction, many elaborating on a refreshing twist: that of hope, optimism, and belief in that ineffable feature that is the goodness of human beings. Mean characters also populate the various settings found in the collection, nonetheless the author's thrust does not relish or idolize cruelty.

On the surface, the stories have what seems simple plots, for example a character desiring his own death, or a group of migrants looking for a better home, or a character looking for the latest drug craze, yet another waking up after a 10-year coma, or two very different post-human species searching for means to survive in a deteriorating world. The author's skill resides in his ability to layer unexpected and original meanings into these plots. The protagonists are fully developed characters whose actions lead the reader on exciting journeys of the possible and probable, now feeling empathy, sometimes distrust, ending with an "aha!" moment which pulls all the actions together and makes reading these stories so enjoyable.

The short story genre allows the author to focus on a particular aspect of technological innovation, especially the one that is not normally associated with advanced AI or surveillance technologies affecting human life. This aspect then becomes the point of ethical consideration. In the story *Fernando Morales, This Is Your Death!*, if a society has the technical ability to stage the death that one desires, is it then ethical to broadcast this death on a reality show even though it is cruel? In *Awakenings*, is the AI surrogate for a mother (who was in coma for ten years) still the "mother" since the AI has all the characteristics of the biological mother? *The Green Ship* gives a solarpunk solution to the migrant crisis in the Mediterranean, allowing technology to pass over political, economic, social barriers and lead to peaceful and humane living. *Midsummer future* imagines a world where infertility is the state-enforced norm and fertility is highly sought-after male characteristic which a woman is able to find through a computer game. *Italianskij tikaj tikaj* and *90 cents* extol the goodness of human beings despite the terrible war facilitated by technological advances in the first and inhuman treatment of children in the second story. *Flush* gives a highly entertaining explanation of what peace and quiet means for an individual in a society which exalts loud noise. In *Celestial formatting* transmigration means moving people's "soul" from one format to another: what if there is not enough disk space to accommodate two individuals who love each other to be together? *The Assassins' Level* treats crimes committed against avatars in role-playing games seriously. *Two worlds* offers a glimpse of two groups of post-human mutants who have to collaborate in order to survive.

Francesco Verso's poetics of imagination allows "potentials and actualizations of humanity" (paraphrasing Darko Suvin's expression) to thrive. Let's hope that there are many other stories forthcoming.

Jana Vizmuller-Zocco
Senior Scholar,
York University
Toronto, Canada

FERNANDO MORALES, THIS IS YOUR DEATH!

translation by Sally McCorry

In primitive societies death is always perceived as the intervention of an actor: an enemy, a witch doctor, an ancestor, or a god. The Christian and the Islamic Middle Ages saw in each death the hand of God. Western death had no face until about 1420. The Western concept of death, which comes to all equally from natural causes, is of recent origin. [...] It was not until the 16th century that European peoples developed the "art of dying well". For the next three centuries peasant and nobleman, priest and whore, prepared themselves throughout life to preside at their own death.

Ivan Illich, Towards a History of Needs

On the evening of October 20th, while he was surfing the net, Fernando Morales discovered how he was going to die. He had been browsing through websites promoting funerary services – some of them even promised the virtual presence of VIPs – when he came across an ad that suited him to a tee.

THIS IS YOUR DEATH:
DIE ON LIVE TELEVISION. YOU'RE NEVER TOO LATE TO
BE FAMOUS!

It was a promo for a popular show, a favorite with the age group Fernando had belonged to for many years. On several discussion forums he read that the participants died peacefully, almost with a smile on their lips, so he saved the address in his favorites.

The price quotes he had collected over the last few months showed that euthanasia cost on average about eight-thousand euros, whereas a lethal dose of sodium pentobarbital cost just twenty. Even an inexpensive cremation cost much more. In a strongly growing sector such as that of the funeral services market, there were alternative solutions.

Fernando called the toll-free number the very next day, introduced himself to the girl at the help desk, and after putting himself forward as a candidate for the program, they settled on a date for an interview. The lady, Irene, whose voice was sugary sweet, asked him some preliminary questions he didn't know how to answer.

"Sorry, but don't you watch us on TV?"

"Actually... I'm asleep by then."

"I see. Anyway, remember to keep the information I asked you close at hand."

Fernando glanced a little worriedly at the notes he had scribbled on his pad.

"Of course, I'll see you tomorrow..."

He closed the palmtop and began looking through some files. Fernando kept everything in order, year by year, in numbered folders. Each folder contained yet more folders of files: healthcare files, tax files, travel files, household utility files, etc. Ada had always insisted that he deal with the bureaucratic stuff.

Fernando scanned some documents into his computer and saved them as PDF files, storing them in a folder he labeled *This Is Your Death*. The list of documents the show had asked for was very long; it seemed strange that so many were needed for dying.

Wearing a pinstripe suit that only saw the outside of the wardrobe on special occasions, now few and far between,

Fernando welcomed his guests and told them to sit on the sofa-bed. The pension he had lived on for the past seven years didn't permit him to live anywhere larger than this 400-square-foot studio apartment on Swan Street, a respectable area, even if it was on the outskirts of the city. First he had had to sell the three-bedroom apartment near Liberty Plaza, where he had lived with Ada for nearly three decades. Now even this studio had its new occupants lined up, a family of three who had already owned the tiny apartment on paper for a few years now, just waiting for him to be gone so that they could move in.

A moment before he opened the door, when the two funerary consultants were already coming up in the elevator, Fernando realized that his shoes were a bit too big. Or perhaps his feet had shrunk. With every step his heels were lifting, as if he were wearing slippers. He didn't want to look silly or appear too clumsy, so he hurried to find a thicker pair of socks.

As he put them on, he resigned himself to putting up with the inevitable irritation that would doubtless be caused by the sweat between his toes. He was ready. His wife had been wont to say, "If you want to look good, you have to be prepared to suffer a little," and fame was worth more than beauty.

The two intermediaries were called Lucio Fugante and Patty (her surname remained a mystery). In comparison to the visits from the delivery boys who brought him books or those miserable pizza guys who only chatted to wheedle a tip out of him, this was a party.

"So, Mr. Morales, how would you like to die?"

The directness of the question made him sit back in his chair.

"I hadn't really thought about it ..."

"In that case, may I make some suggestions?"

It was a rhetorical question, used to introduce a series of elements that would make up the plot of *his* program. Fernando was enveloped by heat, and not just because of his feet.

Lucio Fugante had flashing eyes, and he kept twirling the palmtop's stylus between his fingers with the dexterity of a conjuror. Every so often he touched the tablet, and marked it with green ticks or little red crosses.

Patty, his assistant, was a brunette. Her bangs reached down to just above her eyes. She watched every move her boss made. At regular intervals she raised an eyebrow or lifted a corner of her mouth, she fiddled with her hair, and flared her nostrils, but she never looked at her hands.

"You live alone, is that right? Haven't you got any relatives, grandchildren perhaps?"

"It's small enough in here as it is."

It was a sad little joke. One by one, the members of his family had either been pushed away or ignored. Arguments, misunderstandings, and tantrums had contributed to sweeping away most of his family relationships. Ada could be an angel, but she had also known how to hold a grudge for years, however small the slight. She had chased some away, and the deaths of others had completed the job.

Fernando belonged to the category of men who had adapted to old age, who had given up fighting the weakness of their bodies and never complained about the disappearance of certain pleasures. In other words, men who had made a lifestyle out of resignation, well aware of the fact that the world would continue to move on without them. For instance, Fernando had always believed that the environment should be protected, people's jobs safeguarded, that people should pay their debts and support their families. In recent years, however, he had kept his peace, no longer taking a firm position on any of those subjects. Maybe it was because he was just waiting to die, to step out of the way and abandon all those principles that had always sustained him, wanting nothing more than to just make it through this last stage of his life.

The most he did these days was grumble a few comments to himself while he was watching the news, a wisp of indignation caught between his lips, but what came out was always innocuous.

When he started talking again his voice was more subdued.

"I'm a widower with no children. Ada and I tried, but it never worked out. She had a problem with her tubes ... whatever, even IVF wasn't possible."

It had been years since anyone had asked him about his wife. It surprised him, because speaking her name automatically set in motion a series of nostalgic images, taking him back to when they had first started dating. They had met in a club on the beach. He had been spinning records in a cabana there on the weekends. Salvo, a classmate of his at the university, had leased the cabana for the whole summer and had decided to provide some evening entertainment in the form of a DJ. Fernando, still a beginner, had jumped at the chance. He lugged his equipment from his house in an third-hand silvery-gray beater – an audio mixer, two pre-amplified speakers, plus three portable stands for mounting his black lights and strobes. At the time, he lacked the material resources to fill three hours with music. Sometimes he had to play tracks more than once to make the evening last longer.

Ada loved House music. She was mad about the Jungle Brothers and liked to drink too much when she was out with her friends. Back then she wore loose fitting dresses, light and often short, dresses it was a pleasure to slip his hands underneath.

Fernando had crystallized those memories into a few sharp images, though the details faded a little more each year. Well, the details hadn't really faded, it was just that it took him longer and longer to recall them. Luckily, it was the more recent memories that had begun to vanish most first, but this was gradually spreading backwards to the more remote ones.

"You'll be on your own then. That's no problem as far as we're concerned. It will be an intimate affair."

Lucio Fugante tapped something on the screen of his pad.

"Tell us, is there a particular place where you like to spend time, that's special to you?"

"No, none. I don't go out very much. The traffic, you know? Besides, it's gotten impossible to find parking."

Patty jumped into the conversation. "What about public transportation?"

Fernando made a frown of displeasure, verging on disgust.

Fernando's social life was spent largely on emotional interaction networks, but even putHe could have lied, passed himself off as a distinguished, salt-and-pepper fifty-something and only post old photos of himself, or he could avoid posting any at all, but they were futile precautions. He was always found out when a dialogue started, then dropped or ignored.

Fernando got bored on his own, but with other people it was even worse. He found a certain degree of relief sitting at his computer and communicating with someone he had only just met on the network, when personal exposure was minimal, companionship unstable and fragmented, and he could maintain an illusion of hope. So, Fernando was happy to realize that these people were professional listeners, true experts in dealing with loss and funeral services in their broadest sense.

Lucio Fugante, who Fernando nicknamed "Mr. Stylus," continued chatting, running his fingers over the tablet's screen.

"Has anybody threatened you recently? Any arguments with neighbors that could lead to revenge or retaliation?"

This interview was turning out to be fun, even though he had to dig around in his memory to reply. Fernando leaned back in his chair.

"The condo administrator is a ruffian and a swindler. He insults me every time we bump into each other on the stairs. Only because I wanted to take a look at the books. I was an accountant for thirty years. No-one can get away with certain things under my nose."

To underlined his point, Fernando got up and went over to the radiator to warm his hands.

"Two thousand euros a year for this sorry excuse for heat. You can't tell me that's not highway robbery. Have you any idea how much pension I get?"

"This administrator... is he a violent type? Likely to lose control?"

"He already has! During a condo meeting he almost knocked me to the ground. Oh, he said he was sorry, that he had knocked into me by accident, but I know he did it on purpose. Trying to intimidate me. "

"What happened then?"

"I went to the police ... and filed a report."

"You went to the police for such a small thing?"

Fernando undid the cuffs of his shirt sleeves and showed them a wrist monitor.

"If he dares come to within a hundred feet of me, a signal goes to the police station."

Patty raised an eyebrow, Lucio ticked a box immediately.

"I see, we can count the administrator out. Let's move on... Have you got any famous friends? Anyone who's already been on TV? Someone who might be willing to sponsor or talk about you?"

"When I was a young man I knew *Cocco*, Flavio Coccolato. We started spinning records together, down in Gaeta. We had a blast at the DMC DJ round-ups. Then I had to change track, because I met Ada... When you have a family, you can't carry on with that life. He did though, who knows if he's still deejaying..."

"Coccolato is a well known name. Can we invite him to the ceremony?"

Lucio Fugante looked around him, taking in the large amount of records lining the shelves. Two Technics 1210 turntables either side of a Tascam mixer were positive evidence of the pensioner's DJ past.

"Flavio hates me...Ada was his girl, before she met me."

Mr. Stylus' palmtop received another red cross.

The funerary agent didn't give up, in fact every answer from Fernando seemed to whet his interest even more. There was something slightly bitter and unexpected about the life of Fernando Morales.

"Mr. Morales, is there a place you really dislike? Somewhere that scares you for some reason?

Fernando thought about the question. He knew the answer already, but seeing someone hanging on his every word was giving him a pleasure that had been missing from his life for a very long time.

"Doctor's offices. Every time the insurance company makes me go in for a check-up, some know-it-all specialist would pop up with some fancy new theory, just trying to prove to me how sick I was."

"Maybe it was because of your insurance policy?"

"Exactly, but that's not the only reason. They would talk about diseases I'd never heard anything about. New diseases, they said, those know-it-alls. 'Preventive' diseases, the kind that make you feel sick before you've even gotten sick. Pathognomonies, symptomologies, that's what they called them. I don't know. Is it possible to invent diseases? What do you think? How can *new* diseases exist, if we are always the same?"

Patty decided to chime in again. "But, doctors follow procedures. It's not merely a simple question of form or language. They have rules to follow, rules that everyone agrees on."

"Miss, take a look at me. If this old jalopy and everything in it is destined to die sooner or later, at least give me the pleasure of holding onto the steering wheel when it happens, instead of getting dragged around every which way.

Patty nodded. At the same time as she was noting down his answers, her fingers were tapping out a message on her palmtop. The danger that she might note down some of the information incorrectly, made Lucio glare in her direction. When Patty raised her eyes from the screen, he shot her a look that seemed a warning not to butt in again.

"Please, go on, Mr. Morales."

"I just wish they would leave me in peace. It was the same story with Ada. For a long time I had to wait for her yearly check-up to find out if she was getting worse. Then one day, I started getting daily updates about her tumor on my cell phone. For the hospital my wife had become a kind of time bomb, and they, as a caring health service, kept an eye on the countdown. I mean, is that any way of keeping people informed?"

Lucio nodded, a visibly engaged listener.

"It's as if they give us permission to live only so long as we accept certain courses of treatment. They didn't give a hoot about Ada getting better, they just wanted to prolong her illness. I've not wanted to have anything to do with doctors since. I'd rather die my way..."

The two mortuary consultants exchanged a knowing glance. That's why they were there. A smile appeared on Patty's lips, which she quickly repressed.

Worried that his guests might go, and he would lose all that attention far too soon, Fernando got up and went over to the kitchenette corner of the studio.

"I'm sorry, I seem to have forgotten my manners. Would you like something to drink? Some coffee?"

"Yes, please, a coffee, thank you. And for you, Patty?"

"Me too, thanks. No sugar."

While Fernando filled the coffee machine, Mr. Stylus continued with his questions.

"Now Mr. Morales, I have to ask you if you have ever had any rare diseases? Have you ever undergone any surgical procedures, or do you suffer from any kind of disability?"

Fernando kept his back to the room and thought hard. He was fast understanding the best strategy to adopt with these people. It wasn't like during normal everyday conversation, when it was important not to show people just how sharp and brilliant you were, to know when to keep quiet and listen with the right amount of attention and empathy. On TV, things needed to be handled differently. You couldn't risk people's attention wandering, or allow yourself to appear boring or dull.

Fernando turned and spoke in a mournful voice, implying goodness knows what. "Well ... I'd rather not answer that."

Mr. Stylus made a green tick and added an asterisk as if to highlight a point for further investigation later. As Fernando lit the flame under the coffee machine, he felt an accompanying flush of excitement.

"Have you ever had any problems with the law?"

Fernando walked back and picked up an envelope from the end table next to the sofa. He pulled out a sheet of paper and handed it to Mr. Stylus, who read it quickly.

"Assault? Resisting arrest? What happened?"

Back in front of the stove, watching the coffee pot, Fernando shook his head, aggrieved. "Those bastards at Macroford, they enjoy messing with people. They sell software they know is already outdated. The sales assistant wasn't interested. He just kept saying it wasn't up to him, that re-called versions couldn't be re-ordered or exchanged. They call it "scheduled obsolescence." The fact is, as soon as you begin to work out how to use something, it changes and you have to start all over again. I was so tired of all that hassle ..."

Fernando pointed at a wood bureau, its paint long worn off, on which his guests could see the silhouette of an old desktop computer.

"That computer over there drives me mad."

"Is that why you assaulted him?"

Fernando, interrupted by the sound of the coffee bubbling noisily, did not reply. He took his time fetching two demitasse cups, into which he poured the steaming liquid. He arranged them on a tray with the sugar bowl and spoons, which he presented to his guests.

"You didn't answer my last question. Is there something wrong?"

Fernando grimaced, but said nothing else.

Mr. Stylus went back to reading aloud. "'With a series of punches to the sales assistant's stomach ...destroying a number of 32-inch monitors...and threatening the staff with a walking stick.' Don't you have anything to say about this?"

"What is there to say? We take an average of eighty years to disappear from the face of the Earth. Products only last a few months."

Fernando moved his pointing finger to the right, towards the TV.

"That is an old Zoppas TV from the '50s. It was my grandfather's, and it would still work if there was a signal for it to receive. I mean, we used to hand a part of ourselves down through our possessions. Today things hand themselves down to other things, so no one gets attached to anything anymore. Isn't that a good enough reason to get angry?"

The consultants glanced at each other. He could see they were a little shocked but, in the end, they had to know, with all the elderly people who had passed through the *This Is Your Death* studio, that when you get old it's much better to have a trunk full of memories to hang on to than a pile of money.

Lucio finished his coffee, put his pad down and leaned forward.

"Mr. Morales, between us, what is your biggest secret? Is there something that you would rather no one ever found out about you?"

Fernando sat back down. His expression was meek, his hands clasped over the curve of his belly.

"I'm a simple man. I don't have secrets."

"Come on, don't be afraid. We all have at least one shameful secret, and people are more interested in vices than virtues."

Patty winked in support of her boss's words.

"Well, if you're going to put it like that, I'm a little ashamed about the Palace Motel."

"What do you mean? Can you explain?"

Fernando hesitated for a moment before letting his guard down.

"It's just that, I go there on my own, not in company, and that could be misunderstood..."

"Go on. You can trust us. If there is something special, that might make you famous, we want to know all about it."

"The first time I went there, I went for a couple of days because my home was being repainted. Ada had passed away three years before and I wanted to change the color of the walls. It was our anniversary. The room at the Palace had just been cleaned, but you know...such a run down motel, it's a miracle it has any stars at all. To begin with I noticed little things that made me feel sick, like a blonde hair stuck in a crack between the shower tiles, a woman's handprint on the edge of the mirror, a piece of tissue stained with lipstick caught between the mattress and the box spring."

"So? That all seems pretty standard, for a cheap motel..."

"You don't understand. You see, it was at that very moment that I felt myself become old, as if all my future anniversaries had arrived all together, all at once. It was a slap in the face, the sudden realization I would be excluded from those kind of experiences for ever, from that time forward. But even that isn't the point. When I feel the need for warmth, or when I'm feeling a bit low, I rent a room that has just been vacated."

Patty's eyes widened. Now this was something truly morbid, something that would have viewers glued to the screen. As Fernando continued, Mr. Stylus marked tick after tick after tick.

"It might sound ridiculous, but I've come to the conclusion that those rooms absorb feelings. If you concentrate, you can feel the echoes of lovers coming from the walls and the sheets. Maybe not all their gestures are loving, maybe the place is full of deceit and betrayals, and who knows how many bad feelings and bad things happening. In the end it doesn't matter. I just want to absorb the vibrations."

Mr. Stylus looked extremely satisfied. He saved Fernando's profile on his pad and checked his agenda.

"Alright then, Mr. Morales, we're done here. We'll need a few days to put together the video portion of your Death Notice, which will be broadcast the week before your program. However, I can tell you now how you will die. On November 11th we will come for you and take you to the Palace Motel. We'll have to bend the rules to do it, but in this case I believe it's worth the trouble to film the episode on location. There you will become *famous*!"

Fernando didn't say anything or express his doubts about the choice of location. After all, if he was going to die, one place was as good as another. Besides, the two consultants really seemed to know what they were talking about. If the public would like it, there was no point in insisting they film it at the studio.

"Is there a time slot you prefer? We have two viewing peaks, one in the morning, and one in the evening."

"The morning is better. I usually eat supper early, around six o'clock, sometimes even earlier. Then I can slip on my pajamas, take a Lorazepam or a Xanax, and get under the covers with a glass of red wine, some cigarettes, and a good book."

"Fantastic. There's nothing left for you to do but sign here."

Mr. Stylus held out his namesake and Fernando the signed the program agreement on the screen of the mortuary consultants pad.

After Fernando had accompanied the mortuary consultants to the door, he went back to the kitchen and poured himself half a glass of cognac. Then he sat down on the sofa. It was still warm. Fernando wore a look of moderate happiness on his face. He pressed his fingers against the rough fabric of the sofa. None of his acquaintances had died like he was going to. He sniffed at the back of the sofa and rubbed his cheek against the armrest. Finally, he moistened his lips with the cognac, content with how things had gone.

His colleague Mario Cantini had left this world between his sheets nearly a year ago, and no one had even noticed he had died until ten days later. He was found by a policeman who had come to serve him a six-month-old fine but got suspicious when he smelled the stink from outside the door.

Fernando had only found out about his friend's passing from the status update on his emotional-interactions network profile.

Clara De Amicis, his ground floor neighbor, was only technically alive. In fact, she had been reduced to a green signal on the display of the machine keeping her in a state of "suspended animation". Fernando saw nothing animated in her condition. Anyway, although her children had no intention of pulling the plug, she had already been in some other place for a long time.

He couldn't even remember how some of his acquaintances had died. Recalling all those people made Fernando think that, although medicine had worked hard to prolong life, the last stretch, old age, was still sad, and far too often lacking in any respect for human dignity.

He had no problem admitting that sometimes, for the elderly, death represented nothing more than a sort of liberation. So, in the end, why not make that inescapable event into something positive – like when a child was born? Why not make it into something *spectacular*?

On the last day of his life, Fernando Morales didn't shave. The certainty that, before too long, his body would be decomposing made him lazier and more apathetic than usual. Despite this, he still took the time to remove the hairs from his nose and ears. The action reminded him of Ada, and the intimacy they had once shared. When chance would find them standing in front of the mirror together, they would always tease each other, pointing out those little changes that, over the course of the years, had transformed them, one cell at a time. How many versions of Fernando Morales had been reflected there? He was looking at the last of a series of identities that, though differing one from the other, had all been him.

Then, from the corner of his eye, he saw a look of surprise on his face. They had told him he was going to die today. They had told him he would die on live TV. They had told him he would die in the Palace Motel – but they had not told him *how* he was going to die.

When his doorbell rang, Fernando felt a shiver.

On his doorstep, in addition to Mr. Stylus, he found himself facing a TV crew, armed with cameras and microphones, a set dresser and a make-up artist.

"Good morning Mr. Morales. Have you slept well? Are you ready for your big day?"

"More or less. It is my first time, after all."

Among those people, Fernando felt out of place, a foreign body.

The set dresser took in Fernando's pinstriped suit and laid a hand on his shoulder. "I'm sorry, but this won't do."

Fernando spread his arms helplessly, but the man was already taking the wrapping off a new, tailor-made suit.

"We took the liberty of having this custom-made for you. For your big day."

Lucio shot Fernando a wink and pointed his finger towards the ceiling. For a moment, Fernando thought he was referring to a hypothetical imminent meeting with

God, but then the consultant silently mouthed the words, "It's for the sponsor."

As death approached, Fernando felt much humbler. He changed into his new suit and, when he left his house, he took nothing with him. He shut the door, not bothering with the deadbolt, and followed the others out.

On the way to the Motel, no one deigned to speak to him, not even to offer him a crumb of pity. No one asked him *why* he wanted to die, even though he was still in good health.

When they got to room 1552, the TV crew laid out their cables, plugged in their cameras and arranged the lights so that every shadow was eliminated. The set dresser changed the sheets on the bed and the curtains on the windows. He shifted the furniture around a bit to give the room a semblance of normality, adding a couple of chairs and some fresh flowers. Meanwhile, the make-up artist took care of Fernando's face.

There were only twenty seconds left of the video broadcast about the life of Fernando Morales. Suddenly, the Motel room door flew open and Patty rushed in. Her heaving breast radiated anxiety. She was holding a sheaf of papers covered with countless red circles and underlining.

"Lucio! Quick, come over here."

Patty handed the papers to her colleague, who was sitting next to Fernando. Fernando, who was busy thinking about what he was going to say, barely noticed.

"We checked out his story. We always do, but it took us longer than we expected. Mr. Morales told us a pack of lies. His wrist monitor isn't connected to the police station, it's connected to Doctor Brogli's clinic. The doctor told us that Fernando has stopped looking after himself, he refuses to take any medicines, and appears to be living on alcohol and sleeping pills."

Lucio Fugante sat up straight in his chair, then he leapt to his feet and slapped the papers down into Fernando's lap.

"What? Were you trying to make fools out of us?"

Patty pulled out her electronic diary and pointed it at Fernando.

"That's not all! Mr. Morales here has never even met *Cocco,* as he called him. We telephoned Flavio Coccolato, and he denied all knowledge of Mr. Morales. And there's more. Ada Morales's medical files say that she didn't die of cancer. She died of natural causes on the 23rd of March, 2019.

Fernando hunched his shoulders and muttered something almost incomprehensible.

"I...I wanted... just..."

Patty pointed a finger at him, as if she wanted to spear him with it.

"Even the police report was forged with Photomaker, and the Palace Motel guest register shows that you have never been a client here before."

"That's not true, I have been here before. I watched from outside."

"Mr. Morales! You invented everything! *This Is Your Death* is a serious show. You are a liar."

Fernando was overcome by a feeling of immense sadness.

"I might have lied, but it got you interested..."

"Why did you do it?"

He was no longer listening. Memories he had deliberately left hidden in a corner of his mind were beginning to return.

"I saw Ada die, by my side. In years and years, it was the first time she didn't answer when I called. I called to her for a long time, quietly at first, and then more loudly. We had lived together for so long I hadn't the heart to leave her, until her body became a corpse. The elegance of her face, still intact until her last evening, became unrecognizable after a few days. When she started to smell, she started to scare me. It was only then that I could convince myself that *that* was no longer my Ada. When the ambulance men came, they understood. They felt sorry for me. My neighbors didn't. They started to look at me strangely, suspiciously.

"So, what? You decided to put on this show? At our viewers' expense?"

"No, it's that I didn't want to die alone."

Slowly, Fernando began to rub his feet back and forth against the floor. Then he stamped violently. Everyone in the room stared at him in shock.

"It's not what you think. I'm not crazy. I have an acute mycosis infection on my feet. I have bacterial infections and eczema. Didn't the good doctor tell you that too when you spoke to him?"

Stricken by a kind of frenzy of itching, Fernando kicked off his shoes.

"No, he didn't tell you, because he didn't know how to get rid of it!"

To the horror of all those present, he ripped off his socks.

"I'm sorry, but I really have to…"

Fernando scratched so hard to get rid of the itching that his feet started to bleed. Then he hung his head, slurring pathetic half-finished sentences.

"I wanted to end it all without suffering too much. I've earned that right haven't I, in eighty years of life? I've never done anything to deserve being treated like that. Do you think I can go on like this until I'm a hundred?"

This last question had been directed towards the camera, and that was when Mr. Stylus interrupted Fernando's stream of delirious statements.

"No, Mr. Morales, I can assure you that you won't last that long. You signed a contract and have to die now."

"I know. You don't have to remind me."

Mr. Stylus had not stopped the cameras rolling. The studio had just informed him that their ratings were going through the roof.

"Listen, I'm sorry about your wife, but I've got a schedule to respect. There are other people waiting to die."

During the last part of Fernando's existence, the days had followed each other in mechanical repetition, a copy of a copy of a copy. Appearing on *This Is Your Death* had marked a change in direction, a break with monotony of his present life. Fernando found a small measure of consolation in this, of joy almost, although perhaps that word might have appeared a little strong, all things considered.

"I'm glad Ada isn't here. Even though she drank, even though she was paranoid and took offence easily, she had so much class. If she could see me like this, in this state, I would only have added to her suffering."

Mr. Stylus gave a decisive-sounding sigh. He turned to the film crew.

"All right, call in the coffin people. We're ready here."

"Coffin? What coffin? You never said anything about a coffin."

"That's because we've only just decided."

Fernando hunched his shoulders as if looking for comfort, as if anyone would cry *with* him and *for* him. If Mr. Stylus's choice was a kind of punishment, he didn't think he deserved it.

"So, you know about my claustrophobia."

"Mr. Morales, you may have lied to us about your past, but Doctor Brogli told us all about your problem with enclosed spaces."

Fernando's eyes were suspiciously moist. He sagged in on himself. He felt like a flower whose stem had been unexpectedly crushed. Lying had stripped him of the opportunity to die on live TV with a smile on his lips, in front of a massive audience.

Mr. Stylus read out a clause from the contract.

"In the event that the client should fail to fulfill his obligations, the Studio reserves the right to proceed with burial at its own incontestable discretion, in accordance with the methods and timeframe set forth in point 11 of this agreement."

Two gravediggers lifted Fernando from his chair and laid him into the coffin. They carried him from the Palace Motel room accompanied by an audience that peaked at 13 million viewers.

In the days that followed, public opinion was split into three factions. There were the Euthanasians, who supported the Studio's choice, based on the principle that no one should be able to choose the manner of their own death, since that would be suicide. There were the Moralists, who accused *This Is Your Death* of murder. Finally, there was the Happiness League, who complained about unusual and intentionally pitiable ending.

Fernando Morales was the *mortuary sensation* of the month.

MIDSUMMER FUTURE

translation by Sally McCorry

When it all began, the first time I saw Yumiko's avatar, I had no suspicions whatsoever. Now I know more than anyone should, and not only about her.

It was a morning like any other. I was eating at the Nu-wok restaurant after my nightshift at ReStore. I was so excited that I had eaten too much *wasabi* burning my lips. A voice crooning sugary oriental melodies played over the restaurant's loudspeakers. The food made me wonder what might happen between Yumiko and me: I bit hungrily into the last of four tuna *uramaki* and put the *ohashi* with my initials back into my shirt pocket.

I was going to see her, not just with my eyes. In person.

Chewing, just above my head on the tiles of the chequered blue wall, I noticed a *haiku*. The graffiti writer had used wire from the *nori* wrap of some sushi and coated it with a molecular spray. I recognized it as the one by the zen mater Basho.

IT IS SAD TO PART AT FALL

DIVIDED IN TWO PARTS

LIKE A BIVALVE MOLLUSC

I wet my throat with an Asahi ginseng beer, screwed my takeaway box into a ball, and chucked it in the litter-bin beside Nu-wok's door.

I nodded to Maeko, the checkout clerk. Our relationship was symbiotic, not the usual perfunctory customer-supplier link. She treated me with kindness, with the special care typical of Far Eastern countries. I uploaded the amount for the *Nikko* (Sunlight) menu she had served me and scooted off to my home niche.

I hired an aluminium bike from the Centraal Station dispenser and charged it to ReStore's account. In addition to paying the rent for my single niche, my co-worker contract included a reward for using a low heat dispersion transport for at least 180 days a year. I pedalled nervously dodging other cyclists who complained about my recklessness. The rush hour traffic forced me to jump curbs, dodge between a pair of girls and through a group of students cycle-sailing.

"Godverdomme!"

The old woman swore at my back as I latched onto a tram using my trailer magnet. I never slowed down. The rest of the world didn't know about my date with Yumiko. I had been waiting for it for days and days, and soon I would *interdream* with her. I wanted everyone to disappear and get out of my way.

Yumiko was probably waiting. Her nightshift had ended and our meeting would begin with the new day. We had planned our first interdream together for this special day. Our avatars had been born on the same calendar day so this was Midsummer's Day plus our double birthday. We deserved luxury.

We had been working, Yumiko and I, for six months on the same viral marketing channel. We had never met in flesh. She worked in Sloterdijk, while I was in Amsterdam. We sent "logic bombs" to explode inside the inboxes of millions of potential customers. Explode was our word for the job, not ReStore's. They said we launched *promos,* based on consumer preferences, then we would send the actual pitch and set run away fast. Some think what we do is worse than useless. In reality, some of our campaigns, the very sharp and focused ones, could yield tons of credits for ReStore.

The only bad thing was that if we were caught in the act, that is, if someone managed to trace us all the way back to our IP addresses, our bosses would deny any knowledge of our existence. It was a condition of our contracts that we didn't know who was supplying us with information. I mean, we knew who our bosses were and they in turn knew all about us. However, as the viral marketing team, we were hidden behind our avatars.

The bad guys disseminated commercial traps and decoy offers, limited time sales and progressive coupons across the Net; we played by the rules, even if we were nuisances. Common people were busy filtering messages, to avoid spamming, sniffing and phishing, You may call it promo-war, if you like. To us, it was only believe-and-pay.

So we weren't supposed to use the company hyper-band for chat, gossip or flirting, but we didn't care. Yumiko wasn't one of those whambam girls, or simply flesh-with-a-hole you wanted dump after an interdream together. She never hassled me about anything. We had quiet conversations, sometimes exchanging suggestive banter without ever slipping into vulgarity.

As I cycled toward home, I imagined what it would be like crossing the server clouds and *soaring* together with her after so much idle chat...

Half way along the Damraak I pulled the brake lever, skidded across the rosy asphalt and pulled off at the corner by Albert Heijn's store. I dug anxiously into my bag.

Where the hell was my oneiromantic chip? Had I left it at Nu-wok? I couldn't get back, in six minutes I was supposed to be in my home niche. But there it was in an inner pocket. I slid it straight into the *V-lenses* slot to avoid wasting any more time.

With one click, I accessed the marvels of the dataverse. Maybe it was too soon, but I could avoid carelessness or sloppiness with interdreams. I had no intention letting real life haemorrhage into the middle of experiencing a breath-taking adventure with Yumiko.

After all, what else was the point of interdreaming?

When the chip completed its upload, my visual field was crammed full with data. Layer by layer, everything in a radius of a hundred cubic meters animated and executed a reverse striptease. Reality wore information like clothes and it was sent directly up my optical nerve to my brain. All around me, a shower of shapes started raining down like a sparkling mist. 3D faces of actors and actresses filled every shop window, exhorting me to wear t-shirts and trousers in *pret-holo-porter*.

I hastily pushed back into the flow of traffic and was forced to slalom between the menus of Tex-Mex, China Blue and Eatalian restaurants fluttering along the roadside. I curled into aerodynamic position – head bent down to the handlebars – and dashed between projections of rotating plates, kebabs, and desserts presented as if they were Christmas gifts.

On both sides, gurus with coloured turbans shouted slogans. They gave free advice in a bass didgeridoo tone – a perpetual "hommm" – offering methods of hypnosis to combat the weaknesses of the flesh and other means to help strengthen what in their jargon is called "ethereal resistance".

Every form of abstinence is a form of virtue

They didn't convince me, though. I knew how to practise abstinence. I had interdreaming.

Opposite Rokin a few strip-teasers mimed obscene moves through their windows. The pavement was packed full of bustling tourists trying to rub against their insubstantial images.

Amsterdam was an exploding dataverse!

I paid no attention. Behind the pathetic lace curtains, everyone had their own V-motion to follow. I passed my office, a co-work niche, which I shared with other fifteen free-lancers in the spacescraper before Rembrandtplein. My bike's GPS made my handlebars vibrate. The display warned me of any incoming danger.

TRAFFIC JAM – TURN LEFT NOW – THEN RIGHT

The GPS took me by the canal behind the Amstel, losing me fifteen seconds.

I arrived at Waterlooplein market, where I often came to wander around during the week hunting down the most fashionable *kitschery*.

Three more minutes and I would be late. I stood on the pedals, left the Visserplein roundabout and flitted at speed through the traffic on Muiderstraat. My goal was in sight, fifty meters to my left. I cut across the lane, dodging a Limorcedez armoured car and finally jumped off my bike leaving it to take itself to the dispenser by my door. I swiped my biometric card over the domotic reader at the door and ran, hardly touching the floor.

The lift had already locked on to me, and, recognising my face-scan, opened.

"Welcome, Thomas. Are you in a hurry? Would you like to authorize a nonstop?"

"Good idea... Shut up now though."

As I flew up to the thirty-sixth floor, I swallowed to unblock my ears. Sixty seconds left. I rubbed my hands together and passed them along my trousers. When I came out of the lift, I slid my card into the slot beside No. 3556.

"Lights!" I said, "Open a Grolsch. Priority to the hyper-band and disconnect the rest."

Thirty seconds. Countdowns turn me on.

My home niche was bare. Maximum of minimalism. I fabbed everything in it myself, tools, cutlery, clothes – all the disposables, using a 3D poly printer at the end of the corridor. I was the only real thing in it.

I uploaded myself to the Dreamvision server. My throat was dry imagining how Yumiko might be dressed. I started fantasising about her the moment the Grolsch touched my lips.

Twenty seconds. Usually her avatar was manga sugar for my brain. One third porno hentai, one third gothic harajuku, and the rest in pure apsara dancing style. My enjoyment forecast indicated a very high probability of having an amazing time.

Fifteen seconds. Lying on the Winstron oranje sofa, my domo played, in no particular order, the pop-ups I hadn't blocked: all the previews of the daily series on HOLO, the fridge's list of past-use-by-date food and nutrients to order from the Albert Heijn website, plus the active n-options for my microwaveable nutrition.

"Really K, Really K, Really K."

A golden logo, made from rubbery corn-flakes, appeared on the Dallenkey table. As I flipped it off with my finger, it intoxicated me with a cloud of free promo-steam. Calories, molecular formula and warranty. It seemed like a "logic bomb" by Dirk Van Der Broek, our number one competitor.

I wasn't in the mood for shopping, especially not at Van Der Broek. I just wanted Yumiko. Three, two, one... I was so agitated the incoming call sent me into pre-ecstatic mode.

"Yumiko, Lady of my Dragon... Dead on time, as always."

"Hello Thomas, I've just got back from Sylonia. It was great, they had a brand new chippery."

Her slim body was wrapped in semi-opaque radiation which highlighted her curves. The hip-waist ratio exactly matched my preferences on file. She was using these seductive details to entice me.

"Sylonia? The bioluminescent polder? Do you want to hop over together?"

"Why not? It would be cool to go back there. What about next week? But physically, in the flesh."

"Physically? I need to think about that. What are you doing now, shall we connect?"

"What's the matter, Thomas, can't you wait?"

"Well... No. I meant I am so excited. I ate at Nu-wok so I don't have to disconnect for any meals. My head is bursting for this interdream... Oh, and happy birthday!"

She did not answer, instead her avatar invited me to interlace.

ACCEPT REQUEST TO INTERDREAM WITH YUMIKO

YESNO

I hit the yes. My V-lenses darkened and the domo's surreal tones disappeared in a vortex of pixels. I could feel pins and needles tingling through my body. My mouth fell open. I was waiting for connection overload, like those bible bashers kneeling all-day inside Sint Nikolaas Kerk.

I closed my eyes and waved the world good-bye. Reality doubled, I didn't even try to keep layered visuals. Anyone who could cope with that probably had too much *psilocybe* from magic mushrooms circulating in their veins. I could feel something taking on shape and consistency in the back of my brain... and I was in.

The oneiric filament spiralled, and our heads had started overflowing with interdreams. A continuous greedy rush of experiences ran madly between me and Yumiko. Imagine descending directly in the sentient first person but with the calculation capacity of an hardcore AI. Then disable all filters and any censorship. Pure unadulterated entertainment, in pure privacy. Oxygenate your brain and get ready for take-off.

Destination interdream.

A kind of dense, compact statement of daily living, only much, much more exciting.

Every form of neurosis induced by augmented sociality was wiped away, reset by the interdream vortex.

Ok, we did not touch or sniff each other.

Ok, we did not lick each other, or penetrate, but in interdreams things happen which I defy anyone to imagine.

Here was Yumiko, a dancing divinity moving forward on clouds of music plucking a sitar. Her eyes were eloquent and sometimes she sugar-coated her remote presence with a sweet word and a move. She was sexy and candid. Fluffy yet turgid.

"Relax, let go, embrace the interdream..."

Wherever we were, there were no physical barriers or biological restrictions, we didn't lose ourselves with questions of identity. We were what we interdreamt.

Me and her, us and them, us and him, everything and anything we wished. We chose to be head-to-head, interdream-to-interdream. For someone as anxious as me, that was no small thing.

Yumiko let down her hair and let it fluctuate like the mane of a horse that would never tire of being mounted. Her rice eyes, immense and sincere, were like drops of milk on my lips.

We weren't required to see to believe, nor did we need to listen to understand: we knew each other because we created our own existences. All the places we were in, were created by us as we interdreamt each other: two halves of a symbol, an output *self-magically* re-routed through thousand inputs; a conjunction of senses not requiring the flesh.

King and slave, Lady and beggar, we could be born again and again, taking on whatever forms and appearances we liked most.

The itch in my fingers became a gentle caress and then an oneiromantic exploration, where we interlocked. It came as no surprise when Yumiko and I unlocked the next level of our Kamasutra.

We flashed along a path of draining pleasure. We pick-and-mixed, here and there, from hundreds of erotic experiences. I had her as if I were all the men who had come before me. She had me as if I were her last wish.

Time didn't bother us. Space didn't separate us.

I could not resist a long, amazing *mindorgasm*... and finally I came, neurons exhausted. Who knows how much of myself, of my neurons, I left in Yumiko's.

After this rushing crescendo, the interdream calmed and was gradually subsided.

Yumiko trembled, and faded away. The signal collapsed and we were separated. For quite some time I was left in a state of bizarre sensory detachment. I had the interdream's stigmata burned into my eyes, a silly smile stretching across my face from ear to ear.

"Can I turn the domo back on, Thomas?"

"No, let me rest. Pause everything for twenty minutes. It's in my preferences."

"Twenty minutes have passed already."

I sighed and changed my sweat soaked vest, munched some jellies and thought about doing it all over again next time with the resolution pushed to the limit. I thought about her suggestion of going to Sylonia and of meeting in the flesh. Why did she want that? What could it possibly change for her? I didn't understand it. Nothing was enough for some women.

To its visitors Sylonia was an artificial atoll endowed with vents both above and below the Fuller canopy. Situated in the North Sea, it was thirty minutes away by water torpedo.

I went in person because Yumiko wanted me to although I usually preferred AR experiences. I had been disappointed before by the real thing.

Yumiko's palm was damp and that wasn't the only one of her biometrics out of synch. Maybe she was worried about something or not used to exterior experiences. Even without special effects Yumiko was charming with her sinuous silhouette and enigmatic features.

This time she was dressed up like a vampire. I liked her costume a lot.

As soon as we left the station, I was awestruck.

The immense colonies of bioluminescent worms covering the external walls of the block were like a never-ending aurora borealis. Below, the light reflected by the street was blinding.

I thought we might take a stroll and do a little shopping, but Yumiko led me straight to the Balfour, a *two star* which offered cheap underwater niches.

My satanic little doll knew what she wanted and I was flattered.

I had dressed with care, wearing silver love spurs. I only did this with women I wanted to mark closely.

There were only single-seaters parked in front of the Balfour. There were a few sailing cycles for couples, but nothing else.

The reception display in the lounge projected a hostess avatar who fluttered before us leading us to our sea-floor alcove. She showed us the basic options: scenery corals, Jacuzzi bubble, the brightest worms to light the space. Then she tried to tempt us with Siberian beluga caviar, Amazonian grapes, gypsy orchestras and tribal algorithms composed by a swarm of AIs.

"Do you like it down here?" said Yumiko.

Two meters by five with a wall porthole and sea-view. In a place like this, you could only guess where reality ended and interdream began.

"The view is breath-taking. Everything is so... uncrowded underwater."

But something was wrong. Oblivious of Yumiko's real intentions, I had thought we would have dinner at Kitsch & Chips, sing in a karaoke club, or maybe play a sweaty game of squash, and then recover with a few puffs of skunk. Instead, I saw her undressing in the reflection in the porthole.

Undressing? My mood fell below my spurs. A crescent moon smile crossed her face as she stared at me. For a moment, I thought my SKAMANDER suit was driving her to folly, or maybe my ochre survivor Mohawk, but I was way off track, completely wrong.

"Wait a minute, Yumiko... This could get us isolation."

Off came her shirt, off came her second-skin jeans.

Were the mind-orgasms of the non-incarnated spirit not enough for this mystery woman?

"I know, but I like taking risks."

Risks? This was more like a nightmare.

"And you also know that if they catch us they can keep us in an isolation server for one hundred months?"

Off came her bra, off came her striped stockings.

"Don't tell me a man like you is afraid of making love?"

"Of course not! But I hang on to my sperm. I'm an abstainer."

"I've seen your file on the company channel, but there are no security-cams here. That's why I chose this place. There are only three like it in all North Sea polders."

"Ah, I see now, you like playing dirty."

I was pretending to be tough, but I was scared by what she was risking.

Yumiko rubbed my crotch and gyrated her pelvis like a lap-dancer. I could feel a strange reaction coming from below, a biological erection.

One might renounce the right to procreation, but the arousal response was impossible to control, always ready to surface. It was nobody's fault if I was experiencing a rush of endorphins circulating throughout my body.

We used our tongues until there was nothing left to taste. We investigated every orifice and explored every centimetre of our epidermal archipelago. Still, it was a pity there were so few ways of interlacing physically.

Without penetration, we touched our hips, legs and arms. We rotated inwards, we pushed downwards, then we had each other upwards and by the side.

It was nothing much, compared with the sexual antics of an interdream. No augmented attributes, expanded senses, empathic vortices or strange calculations: nothing at all. To be frank, between Yumiko and me there wasn't even any audio now. Only the moan which escaped from her half-closed lips. Her next words came somehow as a surprise.

"C'mon, Thomas, inside me now."

Oh, shit... This one was really dangerous.

"What? *Inside* you?"

Yumiko was pushing the boundaries. Sexual penetration had been strongly discouraged for years. If you wanted children, if you were unsatisfied by nurturing and hugging a Tamagotchi or bringing up an Avatar, you had to join the waiting list, like everybody else. This was a hard and fast rule which no security-cam would turn a blind eye to. Ever.

I sat there, half erect, waiting.

What Yumiko was asking me to be a part of, with the innocence of a mischievous immature girl, could have serious consequences.

You were only allowed to attempt reproduction after obtaining the necessary authorisation and guarantees covering the request, and even then there were a number of limitations. A basic list of tests and double-checks was required, including positive and negative genetic matching in addition to the usual health checks, and this had to be taken to the social consultant before a request to procreate could be taken into consideration for approval.

There were rules about who could be born.

Some people I knew in Harlemmerweg had ruined their lives for breaking them. They thought it would be no problem, they were convinced that getting pregnant by mistake wasn't so simple. They got thirty months in an isolation server.

"Come on Thomas, you heard me right... Yes, inside me."

Strange impulses were reaching my brain, I liked Yumiko, I might actually be persuaded.

"Yes, but sorry... Why make me your accomplice?"

She fluttered her eyelashes, affecting naivety, at once exciting and excited.

"Because you are different."

"I *am* different. I am the *most* different person around."

I got the impression there was more to this than I understood but Yumiko lifted herself on her elbows and kissed my chest.

"Now, not only different but *special*."

She had a way of saying special that felt like a butterfly caress down my back.

Special? Me? Like when I ordered a *special Lumpia* at Nu-wok? Like when a sale offer was so special that it would never be repeated? It excited me but it didn't ring true.

"Relax, Thomas. People used to do it like this before. Aren't you curious to see what it's like?"

"I'm an abstainer. I don't leave sperm around. It's like a time bomb. Besides I'd be risking a web restriction, and if I can close one more viral campaign, I unlock my holidays and can interdream for a fortnight."

I was imagining police hunting us down, the Ucard instantly withdrawn, my neighbours gossiping about me with every tenant, the sneers of my drinking pals at the Westergas Fabriek bar and then, as a logical consequence, forced deportation to Diemen or some other dismal area of Barbardam deliberately left disconnected from the Distributed Net of Desires. To say nothing of a potential career thrown down the drain.

Doei, doei, future. Bye, bye, comfort.

Yumiko looked like she was about to cry.

"Please Thomas, don't be like this. It's a different kind of pleasure. I know it might seem crude, but it's pure, really. Everyone says it's filthy, but it's not. It's biological, which doesn't necessarily mean it has to go viral too."

The problem wasn't strictly about her, or being frightened of the consequences; it was the idea of a steady relationship that turned me off. I was scared of feelings because if they were intense and long-lived enough, they would dry out my imagination.

It might seem like nonsense, but at the time I was convinced that if this love story continued, it would probably leave me without enough imagination for interdreaming.

I didn't want to make Yumiko angry, so I didn't tell her.

"OK then. If it makes you feel safer, go ahead."

She opened her bag, and produced a blister. Then, before my erection disappeared, Yumiko took my sex gently between her fingers and coaxed it back up again. She rubbed against me, exciting me.

The blister was glossy and slippery. As she put it I remembered our midsummer night, when we were separate as bodies, but united in our interdream. There was something in Yumiko's face, a hint of insecurity, which made me think she was somehow sad. I don't know why, but this made me want to protect her, even though I knew she wasn't a vulnerable person, that she knew all too well how to stay on an even keel.

"If I were wounded, Thomas, would you look after me?"

"If you were wounded, I'd suck out all the poison..."

I was just playing along, but I was still surprised by her answer.

"Here is the wound."

She opened her thighs. She was impossible to resist. This magnetism was different from any interdream, and a little voice inside me whispered that such a "wound" could be the source of thrills but also of disaster.

At the time, I gave credence to the expression *wat je niet weet, doet geen pijn* – what you don't know, can't hurt you

– however, what I learned from this experience was how wrong that was.

Still, this wasn't exactly an offence. It was more a hint of a crime, a half-thwarted crime in embryo. They couldn't send us to jail, or put us in isolation for such a small thing. After all, there weren't even any security-cams... So who cared if and when I chose to let my sperm out?

I hardly noticed slipping inside her. Actually, she did it all, guiding me blindly into her most private place. All at once, Yumiko lifted herself and seized me by the hips pulling me hard against her pelvis. I let out a rough growl.

The vampire bared her teeth and the two Transylvanian-style fangs were at my neck.

"I had them extended. For you."

In my ignorance, I banged my spurs together in pleasure.

"I don't care about the police if I can have you, Thomas."

The fangs she had used on my neck made an even bigger effect lower down in my nether regions. Who would have thought that so little could be enough to alter reality, making it absurd even without V-lenses. I raised the visor from my face, shoving it backwards over my neck. Then I took off the S&F shoes and leather trousers. My momentum built up and I couldn't stop...

"You asked for it, babe. Here comes something *special*."

I pushed, slow and determined.

"Yes, Thomas, you are the special one!"

We grabbed each other by the wrists, but there were no air vortices. In our biological incarnations, the levitation could be explained away by a mixture of hormonal secretions and concentration. Anyway, when I reached her centre it was like that interdream series where a mystical blade is found plunged into solid rock.

I picked up the domotic remote. I needed more stimulation, possibly a *kaiten* tape, like they had at Nu-Wok or something that would take us out of ourselves. Maybe having the bed spin or the temperature drop. I didn't find any controls for that, so I gave up.

Then I tried working out a rhythm, to keep time with my movement. I lost count at once.

This whole thing, this moving inside another body, was strange. Kissing, even passionately, had never taken me to such levels. The use of body and mind together was all very surprising for an abstainer like me. As far as I could remember, kissing was, at its best, a link to another person, not an abyss that you could lose yourself in. It made me fall into a catatonic state, staring at the coffee-coloured beauty spot on Yumiko's sweating face.

A fist of seconds later, I was barely aware of what I was doing, until I moaned with a kind of liberation I hastily tried to repress.

I hadn't given up living protein since *slow times*. I remember with anguish my reaction as a ten year old child, when a virus in the guise of a half-naked striptease artiste appeared on the desktop screen. Theoretically, I knew I shouldn't have watched her; my parents had gone on and on about the risks and told me to close my eyes and turn the computer off if such a thing ever happened. But, before I could use their advice, she had started taking off her underwear and whispering maliciously, telling me to start touching my sex.

At the time I was a young idiot and I hadn't yet learned to abstain.

In both cases the sensation of giving up my sperm was a bitter one.

What Yumiko had said was true, there had been a time when all you had to do to reproduce was interact a number of times. To me, it seemed like a slipshod uncontrolled method of perpetuating the species. Now, that it was done, that we had violated ourselves and the procreation law, Yumiko started teasing me with her nails and I relaxed, emptied.

Strangely enough, my anxiety had gone.

After a while, I opened the door to the Jacuzzi bubble and plunged into it backwards. Yumiko stayed in bed a little longer.

Things changed after that. Yumiko often seemed to be miles away and more than a little strange. She didn't chat as before on the company channel and in Dreamvision her avatar was a shadow on a black background. She avoided connecting and after a week, her domotic channel flat-lined. I didn't know what the matter with her was, but I thought it was absurd of her to ignore me. I didn't consider myself as some "disposable" loser, and I wasn't going to chase after her. I was left with a bitter taste in my mouth.

"Interdream and forget about the rest", was Dreamvision's tag-line, though I suspected it would have been better to self-hypnotise myself instead of beating my head against reality.

Two more weeks passed. One night, coming home after a smoking session with some people I knew in Vondel Park, I found a card on door No. 3556. Its hologram flashed my name.

Dear Thomas, I apologise for disappearing without a word. Rest reassured, it's not what you think. I like you. I like you more than all 2864 boys I interlaced with before you, but they didn't have sperm like yours. None of them did. In fact nobody does anymore. I am going to let you in on a secret only a few people know. You may not like it, and it is unlikely to change your life as it did mine. Everyone is sterile, apart from some rare exceptions. Exceptions like me and, as I found out, you. Only a few people are fertile. I don't know why this is. Maybe we are like those people immune to viruses, or something like that... Perhaps sterility is the result of a biological error, or who knows, maybe it's psychological, a social phenomenon or something. The rate of fertility in women has been decreasing steadily for many years. In fact, very few children are born anywhere in the world anymore. Maybe this is why we are pushed into using the V-lenses so much... Once again, who knows. It could also be related to the procreation lists. I think the Procreation Office people believe that having mapped the human genetic code humanity could finally take control of its biological evolution, so that they see sex as a useless, old-fashioned and even dangerous thing.

"Perhaps what I have done will appear to you to be a horrible trick, a ruse to steal your sperm. Nonetheless, I hope that you won't be angry with me. I am not looking for help or asking for pity. I just want to explain how the desire for a baby, to give birth to a new creature, has taken over my life. I was so frustrated at having to wait... I can tell you now, I was number 1,630,345 on the Procreation list. In practice, my turn would have come thirty years from now at the age of 72! And I don't want to be the mother of a child who could be my great-grandson, like those old mammoths you see so often. I chose you for this reason, Thomas. And for this reason I had to leave not only the job at ReStore but my whole life. If I am caught with an unauthorised pregnancy I don't know what they will do to me. Well, that's not true but I dare not think about it. I have to leave Amsterdam, run away and find a place where I can rest before I give birth. It won't be easy, alone and hidden but I know that other women before me have succeeded, which means that in theory, I should be able to do it too. I don't know how you will feel when you realise that in a few months you'll become a father. I don't know about you, but I can't stand the idea of having just one life...

Yours, Yumiko

After listening to the message I went into my home niche. I downed a Grolsch and then a second. I was on the verge of calling someone, but I thought better. Maybe I should ask for help. Instead, I decided to sleep on it. I didn't need anyone's advice. I knew all too well what to do.

First thing the following morning, I registered as absent on ReStore's server using my V-lenses. I took a long shower and dressed up as I had done few times in my life. An anthracite suit, shiny and light with black linen trousers. I wore my best shirt, the ivory one by H&M with a V-shaped neck, and I chose my most impressive shoes with reinforced heels.

As if in a dream, I cycled across the Amstel and turned up the Herengracht canal. I left my cycle in the rack, softened my mohawk and entered the Procreation Office.

I handed my card to the hostess sitting at the reception desk.

"Good morning Mister Vorek, what can I do for you?"

This beautiful freckled girl with amber eyes caught me off balance with her seductiveness. Generally I preferred more exotic women, but a Dutch girl raised on *stamppot* and *friets* could still hit me where it counts. Ignoring these distractions, I focused on my goal. For a person in the state of mind I was in after receiving Yumiko's message, this wasn't easy.

"Well... I am here to report someone."

She looked at me with sympathetically. She didn't seem anxious, so maybe this wasn't serious. Possibly.

"Where do I need to go?"

With my right hand I held on tight to Yumiko's card stuffed in the back-pocket of my trousers.

"Then go up to the sixth floor please, room 11."

As I waited for the lift, I noticed a couple of girls with big bellies bursting over their trousers. They had containment bracelets on their wrists, and behind them a couple of policemen were keeping them under close surveillance. Their eyes were bright with tears. It hurt to think of Yumiko ending up like this.

It occurred to me that my actions didn't always match my thoughts.

I hadn't erased her domotic address from my e-diary, or blocked her avatar from my Dreamvision channel. Two choices which might appear ambiguous to the Procreation Office people, who were suspicious about everything.

I psyched myself, took a deep breath and entered the lift. On the sixth floor floating 3D arrows pointed me to the room. The sign at the end of the corridor said occupied.

I sat down on a yellow chair. There was no queue and no chance of a bit of idle chat. I took out Yumiko's card and stared at it. Where was she now? How was she getting on?

The sign changed to available. I quickly shoved the card in my pocket and stood up.

Room 11 was a clean and spotless reception area. I leaned over the counter, trying to get noticed by a clerk wearing a cap. His eyes were distant as he punched the air of a holoboard.

"I am here to report somebody."

"Yes, I am listening. Who is it?"

I raised my chin.

"Myself."

His fingers stopped moving and he looked askance at me. "Ok. Why?"

"I have discovered that I am *not sterile*."

Mr. Cap nodded, as if he had heard it all before.

"I understand. Have you any proof?"

"Well, yes. I brought... this."

From the pocket of my suit, I dug out the small pot holding my living swimming sperm and handed it to him.

"You can check this. It's fresh, I produced it this morning."

"We'll do it, Mister Vorek. But I must ask you *how* such an idea ever came into your head."

He gave me a form for the report.

"Please, check my sperm and you'll see I am right."

"Relax, I believe what you say is true. Sometimes, though not often, *anomalies* do occur. That's why we are required to ask you some questions. It's lucky there are still honest people like you around."

"Will you sterilise me then?"

I stared for about three seconds into the form for the eyescan, and then gave it back to Mr. Cap.

"Of course that's a given. I must insist though, how can you be so sure you are not already sterile?"

I looked around nervously. It was obvious Mr. Cap wouldn't let this go. I had to answer but I had no intention of showing him Yumiko's message, of unveiling <u>her</u> secret and causing her to lose the baby. Our baby. Even if she had deliberately conned me out of my sperm to create a child, subverting the procreation lists, I wouldn't give her away to save myself.

"Well, that's not so easy to explain. I... I had an interdream."

"An interdream?"

"Yes, there was this lapillus travelling inside me. Suddenly, I don't know why, it started darting this way and that and then it expanded into a big rotating egg cell. It was malformed, horrific... Then this amorphous being transformed, it grew hands, feet and all the rest. It grew and grew, and in a few weeks' time it became a fully formed baby."

"Mr Vorek, what you are saying is very unusual. What kind of oneiromantic chip you were using during the interdream? Were you by any chance connected to anyone else?"

"Me? No, I was alone. I use a standard Foxconn 6.0 on Quanta V-lenses. I have never missed a new issue of chippery in my whole life."

Mr. Cap wasn't typing anymore.

"Which oneiroteque were you in when this interdream commenced?"

I struggled to keep the ups and down of my biometrics in check. If my bluff didn't work, I risked becoming Yumiko's accomplice.

"I think it was... the one on the canal, along the Singel. Yes, it's called Lothian. Sometimes I have *fun* there. It happened there... Listen, I just want to be like anyone else. No more, no less."

"Yes, but I need to check some facts. Standard procedure, nothing to be worried about. We don't often come across a *fertile* man."

He paused, giving me the chance to say something that would betray me. When I didn't take the bait, he resumed chatting.

"We may need to contact the suppliers you have indicated to clarify whether or not there was a hardware or software glitch. You must admit your interdream sounds really peculiar."

Another pause, as if he hoped I would say something, anything that would give me away. I said nothing.

"All right then. We'll need to go isolation for processing. Just a formality."

Isolation? All I wanted was to get back to my home niche. All I wanted was to interdream some more.

Mr Cap had bought my story.

As I write these words, I still face eighty months in an isolation server.

Italianskij tikaj tikaj

translation by Tom Crosshill

On early February, in the Field Hospital where I was working as a freelance medic, the Major gathered everyone and told us that the enemy troops, victorious in the skies as well as on Ukrainian soil, were heading straight to us. Within three days at most they would reach us.

The Command Area had repeatedly refused to bring seriously injured people to the rear on transport drones. The situation was critical and we medics had to make do with what there was. The costs of war fell on cheap humans first and then on expensive military equipment. The Engineers working on 3D Printed spare parts had five times our resources for medicines, artificial replacements and prosthetics. That's why the Major suggested that those of us willing should make a long march backwards through humanitarian corridors to escape the attack.

Sixty of us accepted his advice. Our group – The Seventh Healthcare Unit – was made of Italians (the local people called us *malienki*), but most of us had Ph.D.'s in medicine and many years of field experiences. There were also hired personnel that once worked as farmers, hairdressers and teachers who had had an online first-aid course before being sent here to deal with cases of otitis, gingivitis, bronchitis, pneumonia, and lower limbs frostbite of second and third degree.

They supplied each of us with a few nutraceutical biscuits and six small boxes of STAMEAT, "the world's most tender beef." It was meat indeed, even though it came from yolk stem cells grown in a tub.

I scanned the RFID product codes with the built-in player of my survival backpack, then summed up the nutritional values. The energy balance – based on an estimate of burned and ingested calories, taking into account the cold and assuming a sustained trend – would secure me nine days of autonomy. Twelve at the most if I slowed down my pace. After that, I would have to find other sources of nourishment.

At my touch, the molecular structure of my clothing thickened. It resembled wool now, like the clothing my mother used to sew for me when I was a child. Thick socks, long underwear, gloves and balaclava, all integrated into a single suit. The shoes, in contact with the snow, repelled moisture. My feet were warm, despite the cold.

When we gathered in the open space of the military field, our handshakes and movements were clumsy.

"Ready to join the scuba divers?" asked Carlo, a red bearded mercenary from the mountains of Friuli who was near to having paid for his house in Croatia.

I nodded towards the forest. "Yes, but instead of water we've got all that snow to dive into."

He shook his head. "You sorry little Roman kitten, winter without snow is like a steak without gravy."

Unlike the others, Carlo said many times that he felt all right in this hellish weather. As a mountaineer he knew how to hunt in the woods and could survive a long time on his own. It would have been useful to follow his footprints. The night temperature went from 20 to 35 degrees below zero, with peaks of minus 44. On the front lines, where the battle was still raging, there were between 70 to 160 frozen corpses of combatants whose military suit had been ripped.

As soon as we started to march, we received notice that enemy drones had started to bomb the airport and the northern outskirts of the city. Some distant rumbles confirmed the approaching danger. We sped up the departure without much talk. The initial direction was easy to take. Our faithful backpacks, mounted on exoskeletons rechargeable by our own walking, followed us on both sides. They were our only source of defense and survival.

The local people we left behind shouted in Russian, a language that for many centuries had been the cause of strife in the region: "Italianskij, tikaj, tikaj!" (Italians, run, run!)

We walked a forced march for five or six days. We ate at least half of our food. When we passed some control station, we didn't receive even the minimum necessary to avoid starvation: there were no more biscuits, nor canned goods to spare. There was nothing left, just snow in a frozen world.

One night we camped on the edge of a forest.

"Ever heard the story of those guys who ate each other to survive?" asked Riccardo in his heavy Southern accent. His wife had left him for a jockey, the famous Remo Mereu, who rode Centaur, the horse Riccardo often bet on at the races. When his wife packed her bags, Riccardo realized too late that she had "bet" in a different way and had won. So he enrolled in the Hiring Fire in hopes of meeting a *devochka* in Ukraine with which to start all over. He often quoted parts of an old movie, "The Sunflowers", where a woman went to Russia to look for her missing husband only to discover that a girl found him in a sunflower field and saved him from freezing to death. He then became her lover out of gratitude. That was another war and those sunflower fields were gone, replaced by transgenic crops.

"If we're going to eat each other, we better get to it before we freeze," I said, and unwrapped one of the last biscuits.

Riccardo did not freeze. Instead he had met a combat drone, 3D printed by the enemy and remotely controlled by videogame pilots. This meeting had been his own end. As they took him to me to the Field Hospital he was shouting, "I didn't see it coming! I didn't see it coming."

He never had a chance. He had only one arm left.

The "remote pilots" won the war. They did it sitting in a chair; they did it thanks to an online crowd-funded campaign underwritten by millions of people supporting the rebels' independence.

Our best airborne and on-field technology couldn't compete with anonymous Big Data zealots.

On the seventh day we encountered a column of NATO mechanized units, led by snow removal trucks that cleared their way. We kept waving them down and asking for a ride; each time, the commander cited strict orders and didn't want to take us aboard. As a private peacekeeping contingent that carried no flag, we were mavericks, more a hindrance to be fed than allies to be assisted or even simple human beings to be carried away from the killing zone.

Some gave us dirty looks, probably thinking the worst of people walking with their backs to the frontline. Then I noticed the badge on their uniforms: STAMEAT CORPS, and felt a knot in my stomach. We told the truth: the Major ordered us to return on our own to escape a sure death.

The commander suggested that we should disband, scatter and stay at some farmer's *isba* for the time being.

"You're just a bunch of mercenaries in disarray, a target too easy and attractive for click-and-shoot," he sentenced. He had almond-shaped eyes behind the balaclava. If the Major was still alive, he would have enjoyed the arrival of fresh, expendable soldiers. Finally he climbed down into the vehicle's cabin and when he re-emerged he threw a few packs of smuggled cigarettes at us.

My traveling mates scrambled to pick them up. I took the chance to observe our group with fresh eyes. We had lost a lot of people; only thirty remained.

That night, we smoked together, sitting in a circle. For the first time, the idea of desertion snaked in. No one said it openly, but our eyes had changed.

If staying together had been our strength so far, now with each day passing by, the idea of splitting up became more attractive. Every night, without telling anyone, some guys took the solo flight hoping to have better chances to stay alive.

Every night fewer and fewer backpacks remained in our circle.

I was a freelance medic, not a mercenary. Yes, I was at the front, but with my Empathic Quotient I had been assigned to Healthcare Operations. The idea of escaping, though inviting, presented challenges in my case. As soon as the news leaked and the contractor found out, I would not get any job in any other war zone.

Yet, to get another job, I'd have to survive this one first.

We were all thinking the same thing.

The next day, I packed without rushing and then, as we were marching in the morning mist, I slowly slipped to the end of the column. At the first opportunity, right before crossing a hill, I unhooked the backpack and disabled the tracking GPS signal, leaving the group.

At first my loneliness felt like freedom.

Ever so often, I followed the backward trails of some unknown mechanized columns. I was afraid of any figure passing along the roadside but, more than anything, I feared the "invisibles", enemy soldiers with camouflage uniforms, who used nanotech to vanish among the silver birches and the deadly whiteness of the snow. They looked like hovering ghosts. The local people, back at the camp, had known them well; they were given a name from Russian folklore – *Leshi*, Lords of the Forest. And yet, cold was the most dangerous enemy I had. Not so much for myself as for the backpack. Every night I had to prevent the joints from freezing, scraping ice chippings and using oily spray over the tissue as not to scratch it. To do a good job, I had to take out my gloves and use my hands until I couldn't feel them anymore. Only then it was the backpack's turn to fix my aching body with its warm shelter as it finally opened itself above my head in a protective little dome.

For days, I barely opened my mouth. Whenever I spotted a distant figure, I laid in the snow. Whenever I received a patrolling drone signal, my only concern was to escape its reception perimeter. So I followed jagged, broken trajectories – walking with but a slit open in my balaclava.

Often, drawn in the shining starry nights or crystallized in icy leaves, I saw my mother's figure. During the first days, her imaginary silhouette gave me little comfort but from the eighth day on, I drew strength from it to move more forcefully.

Sometimes I advanced without any clear direction. The land was all made of a thick white with stripes of grey coming and going into my useless view. There were no clear indications, at most a few downed signs still written in Cyrillic. Even the vehicles' tracks got covered by the snow. It was almost like that old fairy tale the local people used to tell us: every night *Kikimora*, the wicked wife of *Leshi*, left her house in the shape of snowflakes to erase all traces. General Winter had two extraordinary commanders.

The morning was as empty as it was white.

After ten days' march, exhausted and hungry, I spotted the outline of a village. I couldn't tell anymore if it was hope or desperation that moved my steps. As I cleared a road sign from snow, I read Khorol – Хорол.

I chose an *isba* from whose chimney came a wisp of smoke and knocked on the door. A girl opened the wooden door. Cast away from cloud network, I couldn't use any real-time translation app. As I tried to make myself understood, her mother arrived, tears in her eyes, clutching a piece of bloody flesh. Pointing to the flag symbol on my right arm, she said to her daughter, "Italianskij! Italianskij!"

Gesticulating angrily, she explained to me that a couple of days ago she had hosted two Italian soldiers. During the night they had killed and dismembered a calf; then they had fled.

I was offended and upset. Not so much because I felt guilty, but because I was Italian. With inventive gestures, I asked her what they looked like, if they wore special uniforms and if they had backpacks like mine. She put her hand to her chin and gestured a long beard.

I didn't ask any more, fearing to provoke her – fearing what she might do to me during the night. Sleeping with open eyes would have been worse than staying outside, only protected by the backpack's deployed tensile-structure.

The mother raised one finger, indicating just a single night.

Luckily, the next morning, I discovered that the terrible news of the quartered calf had not spread among the locals. I went to the other side of the village and knocked at another *isba* door. An old man looked at me saying nothing. Then two kids appeared between his legs and they smiled at me. Immediately an old woman came up to the door to see what was happening and soon the whole family talked the matter over.

I smiled back at the children and so I was offered a place inside by the fire.

I wondered how many days I had managed to extend my life expectancy.

This family was not afraid of me. I had neither a gun nor a knife: I was no longer a soldier, just a man adrift. On one arm, under the Italian flag, I wore the Red Cross armband that the older people immediately recognized. I had stolen it from a seriously injured man whom that symbol hadn't saved.

From the kitchen, I smelled something delicious. The children took my hand and guide me there. I peered in and saw two women: the first was cutting up half a cabbage into small pieces, the second was browning the other half in a pan with *semichki* oil. On the table, next to a large bag of sunflower seeds, there were four potatoes, a carrot, a piece of dried meat and wild mushrooms.

Touching their chest with dirty hands, they pronounced their names out loud: Tanya was the mother, hazel eyes and grey hair tied together with a bone fork, and Zhenya the daughter, a lock of brown hair slipping out of her veil. When I also pronounced my name out loud, "Cesare", they invited me to sit at their table and share their meal.

To me, after fasting for days, it was all splendid.

I ate *borscht*, some bread and beans. The soup had a blood-red color because of the beet; pieces of grated meat floated in the broth and I didn't think twice before bringing the spoon to my mouth.

"Ochen korosho." (Very good)

I made sweeping gestures of appreciation, typically Italian.

Tanya got up from the table and opened an old cupboard. She took a jar, holding it in her hands like a treasure chest. She opened it and poured a few drops of sour cream into my bowl. Those sour spots made the soup turn to a golden brown. I ate more slowly to thank her, tasting the soup instead of just eating it.

To drink the old man whose name was Piotr gave me a decent wine, made with apples that reminded me of Italy. In return, I offered him a cigarette, and received a small glass of *samagonka* – a home-distilled vodka – that warmed me like I'd never been on Ukrainian soil.

After dinner, the vigil around the fire was short; they asked me where I came from, I mimed a bombing. No, they meant what city.

"Roma! Colosseo!"

They smiled and we drank one last time – the nightcap. Then they noticed my fatigue and pulled out a mattress, laid it in the living room by the fire, and gave me some blankets.

Dinner, wine and the warmth of the fire eased my sleep.

In the morning, Tanya and Zhenya were already working in the kitchen. We exchanged a greeting: me in Italian, they in Russian.

Then, Tanya came up and handed me a package with two pieces of dry bread for the journey. When I got up to thank her, I saw tears in her eyes. So I asked her in broken Russian: "Mama, pocemù plakal?" (Mom, why cry?)

From a near drawer she took out some photos. Among them she chose one and said, "Vot ohn moi sjn voiennji." (This is my son – military) "Dolgoie vremia niet isvesti." (No news a long time)

I comforted her and hugged her. This little enclave of Ukraine would be freed soon, it didn't matter by whom. These people were also made of flesh, though they didn't have a badge to prove it, only the land that nourishes and supports them. In any case, sooner or later, someone would send a letter to this woman.

I stood there in silence, with that family, as if I were one of them, the soldier who had not returned home.

After breakfast, I prepared for departure. I thanked everybody for their hospitality, but when I opened the door, I was discouraged. Leshi and Kikimora together were unleashing a storm of snow. The wind slammed the door against my hands. As I made the first step outside, something held me back.

"Podozhdi." (Wait)

A young woman with bright blue eyes and a pitch-black fringe of hair under her veil was holding me by the arm. I didn't see her the day before. The elders gestured me to stay longer. It was not time to go. That gesture filled me with emotion and gratitude.

I went back inside. Then I noticed the belly of the mysterious woman and I understood: she must be nine months pregnant.

"You are Cesare. Parents said me. I am Lena."

Due to her condition, they must have brought her dinner to bed the night before. The soldier who had not returned – in addition to being Tanya's son – must be also Lena's husband.

"Yes, I am Cesare. Nice to meet you, Lena."

When she smiled, I forgot even my need to go back to Italy.

The children's little round faces, the kindness of these hard women as they went about their household chores, though so far from my own reality, made me feel at home: not the two-room studio in Rome, but in a house full of family life.

Suddenly, the bloody images of war were swept away. They disappeared like drones vanishing in the sky, like bodies hastily dumped in mass graves, like civilians turned into refugees within a few kilometers of disputed territory. Now, even the men of the Seventh Healthcare Unit and the

STAMEAT CORPS mercenaries could be anywhere, transformed into anything.

Every war was *their* war; a war of skilled pilots and brave commanders, cynic politicians and invisible suppliers. But no war is really *ours*; a war fought in our neglected name.

"How could it be to live like that... A simple life, full of frugality," I thought.

I went to the window and pulled back a heavy curtain. The flickering flakes prevented me from seeing much of the village. Only my backpack – turned off and left outside by the barn under a mound of snow – reminded me of who I was.

When the storm subsided, I went out and brought it inside. As soon as I put it near the fireplace to remove the ice, the children looked at the backpack like it was some alien handicraft. They didn't dare to touch it, so when I re-activated the GPS tracking system with a long beep, they jumped back.

Though I had a plan, I knew that it could have not been enough.

Lena poured me a cup of tea from a round-shaped metal samovar representing hairy *Domovoi,* a protective spirit of the house, and I wondered if the way back home could have been shorter than expected. For the first time in many days, the future seemed not so soaked in white. It tasted of sweet and sour pickle she was putting in my hands to eat.

While I waited for the backpack to load its program, I went to the kitchen where Tanya and Zhenya were washing more cucumbers in the sink.

"Shto delayesh, mama?" (What you doing, Mom?)

They pointed at the same pickle I was eating while sipping tea.

"Augurzì." (Cucumbers)

Although we spoke different languages, we both ate with the mouth.

A continuous sound signaled that the backpack was ready to be traced. Instead of pushing the button, I took it, and threw it in the fireplace; it burned well and kept us warm for a long time. In the afternoon we scattered the ashes in the snow outside.

90 Cents

translation by Sally McCorry

The station was crowded even on Saturday. Hundreds of commuters gathered along the platforms and inside the carriages of local trains. Sleepy faces with an air of resignation: there was something mechanical about them, something that made them look more like packages – waiting to be delivered to their final destinations – than human beings.

Clara, even more anxious than usual about my departure, had decided not just to drop me in front of the station, but instead she parked the car and insisted on coming with me up to the coach door of the train for Milan. From her point of view, a distance of a hundred kilometres was an abyss: her anxiety alarm would go off if I didn't answer her vocally within ten seconds, and real worry would obviously set in beyond twenty kilometres of physical separation.

"Call me when you get there, don't forget."

I freed *my* suitcase from her grip and said a hurried goodbye.

"Yeah, yes, I'll send you a text..."

The Mandarina Duck suitcase was not as heavy as it looked in her hands.

It might sound exaggerated, a feeling bordering on ingratitude even, but my mother had the same effect on me as vitamin tablets. I mean, while I was little, vulnerable and fragile, I needed them for strength, to stop me getting a nasty cold, but now that I was an adult, that I've had enough of them, I was getting indifferent. It wasn't just an economic principle, but also a universal rule, a theory of *emotional* marginalism applicable to a wide variety of situations. And because such a theory is fundamentally true (the more you get of anything, the less you appreciate it), then it must also be refutable, (not every mother's love declines the more she gives you, but for mine it was).

As I see it, the terms and conditions of our relationship, and not just ours, should be regularly renegotiated, even though she always turned a deaf ear to that argument.

"Goodbye then, Roberta... Have a good trip and have fun!"

Clara's voice always had that tone somewhere between weary and nagging, especially at the train station. She took off her headscarf to be ready for the ritual goodbye.

There were no tears; she saved me from that embarrassment, at least.

As soon as I got on the train, I looked for her on the platform through the window. She was there down below both hands raised to the sky. This was a new ritual. She usually waved the headscarf in the air, from side to side, as if to catch me and bring me back, whereas this time she looked like she was trying to invoke some mysterious benign force, a protective entity, a good omen to watch over me and protect me from the dangers of a weekend in a different city.

Those attentions, including my father's usual generic advice, didn't really bother me, they were just out of place given that I was 26 now. That was the reason why, every time I went to visit my aunt I always felt a bit lighter, even though she wasn't really living in an amusement park.

Over the last two years, and this was all my own fault, I hadn't been to see her at all, not even on a brief visit. I had been too busy with all the usual silly little distractions. Amongst the less fickle of these was getting my correspondence degree in Economics from the University of Bologna; then I had started working on projects for DEBILON, a debt collection agency: I was hired as a "bloodhound", let off the leash every time a client was added to the list of defaulters. As if that wasn't enough, I had also attended a three-week specialisation course in "Analysis of Ash Bonds", the latest sore in the rounds of high devaluation Bonds. Not that I understood much about Finance, but since part of my salary was in stock option mode it was a good way of trying to understand how to survive and above all defend myself from the attacks of "door to door" financial promoters and the swindlers hiding behind the hundreds of emails disguised as commercial offers.

Thinking about it, all that time must have passed in a different way in the city compared to my small town. Were my parents trying to put me on my guard against urban changes?

My aunt lived in Milan, a city that, according to newspaper headlines and TV shows, seemed more than any other Italian city to be dominated by an *anarchy-banking* system where "urban concessions" coincided with districts administrated by generous bank counters and protective financial institutes.

Since the branch of a powerful Russian bank had taken up residence next to my aunt's house, the Moscova District had been renamed *Sberbank*. I don't mean it had got itself a nickname, or a playful reference, it had officially been renamed by the town planners. Anyway, for the many Russians living in Milan, changing from Moscova to Sberbank wasn't really such a radical change.

The video wall at the end of the coach was broadcasting more ads than news; or rather, I had the clear sensation that the news itself was excessively and openly concerned with various advertising campaigns.

The workers of the luxury brand GdF, in this case not the Financial Police (Guardia di Finanza) but the fashion house "Guccio da Firenze", were on strike. A new shopping centre with a view over the "Renaissance" bridge in Venice had just opened. There had been an accident involving a Porsche and Land Rover "Defender". The Porsche turned out to be the losing party due to "the absence of a strong and reinforced chassis" as the journalist put it.

I turned my face to the window, lost in thoughts. Usually when I travel, or go from one place to another, I start looking behind me. I don't mean with my eyes, but with my thoughts. I realise this might seem a little ridiculous, but that's what happens, the more I move forwards physically – whether I am walking, driving, or sitting in a train, it's all moving towards another place – the more my thoughts wind back on themselves and I, following that backward motion, start to remember things.

Aunt Nancy's husband left her for the hazy figure of a girl from the south – he was a bit of a crook and it's not even worth mentioning his name; to buy himself a large boat he first moved his factory from Brianza to Shenzhen in China and then "deported" thousands of rice field labourers, even getting himself a gold medal from the Institute for Foreign Trade as an Industry Captain in the process. Since then, almost ten years ago now, aunt Nancy has lived in a kind of dismal solitude, holed up in her home, always on her own, with her old pooch of a cocker spaniel.

All this business convinced me that Nancy didn't really have good taste in choosing her companions, and I liked the idea of improving, even if only temporarily, her state of rich miserableness. Yes, rich, because my aunt had half of her husband's wealth in an "anarchibank" account index linked to the shares of Smart-Up Companies (start-up companies whose rate of innovation grows faster than their profits), and lived on the income in a small villa with a front and back garden.

Outside Milan's Central Station, beneath a sky so gloomy it almost looked as though it were made of glass ready to shatter at any moment, I managed to grab a taxi to take me swiftly to aunt Nancy's house.

"Where're ya goin'?"

"Via Bramante, in Sherbank."

The car was a dilapidated TATA driven by an old Venetian guy who chattered happily as he drove, he also managed to make the old jalopy rock and pitch as much as a gondola on the canals of Venice. While he talked, and talked, and talked, I saw rows of signs for numerous Bank Hotels, chains of Hotels especially devised for insolvent clients who were "guests" in there, until their pending credit problems were extinguished.

It worked like this: all those who exceeded their overdraft or missed a repayment instalment, were considered criminals, real criminals, and as such were detained to prevent them from vanishing off or committing a "bankycide", a term used for those who were faking a financial death as a way to escape their debts.

At DEBILON I have managed to catch quite a few of these cunning people but lots of poor wretches too...

I just did my job and sent payment injunctions that could be "spent" (some said "converted") into a number of days in a hotel, but which – in case of prolonged defaulting – frequently became a ticket for the Bank of San Vittore[1], where things were more than slightly different.

This phenomenon, seen from a distance or behind a PC screen, looked like an ingenious if perverse version of Monopoly.

Actually, Milan had changed since the last time I had been there; transient and elusive, it remained a demograph-

---

1 San Vittore is a jail in Milan

ic enigma and it seemed more like a socio-economic vortex than a town, a vortex spinning around the systematic renewal of the inhabitants. The only aspect that had remained intact was its innate productive orientation fed by a collective sense of dissatisfaction and plaintive narcissism, unchanged for centuries.

Milan to cross; underneath on the subways, at ground level on the roads, and now even through the sky: small heliports had sprung up on the tops of the skyscrapers providing jet-packs for the most urgent financial movements.

Milan to live in; with hundreds of minorities, localised hybrids and anthropological mutations. Even though I hadn't seen much of this world first-hand, I had done enough web research, read enough blogs, tweets, and feeds, to have my own idea, though vague and a little abstract, about the city scene, its tendencies, and even the drifts to keep away from.

Paying the taxi driver, I got out of the car and saw my destination. At Nancy's gate I rang the bell and waited for my aunt to appear under the porch. At five in the afternoon, night's darkness had already taken away what little light the clouds had been letting through.

Behind me I noticed some figures in the swirling mist; street kids playing with long infra-red devices like laser swords emitting swathes of light against the wall. The wakes they left behind them traced trajectories and coloured sections on the wall, only to vanish a few seconds later. The wall was alive with moving images.

I guessed it was the latest fashion in urban play-art.

Then the scene went out. The kids suddenly stuffed the strange joysticks into their pockets and ran off in a hurry.

I had the sensation I could see a form in the mist, like when someone has fun guessing at an image reflected in rippling water, except in this case the shape was real. It was making a metallic noise; something was rattling against the ground.

I turned back towards the house and saw my aunt standing in the doorway, her copper coloured hair sticking out from her head like a flaming explosion.

"Roberta! How lovely to see you… You haven't changed at all. Come in, come in quickly smallstuff."

Smallstuff was a reference to my eternally adolescent appearance; fine bones and the same weight as a kid. I moved quickly across the garden where the exotic trees planted by my uncle about twenty years before were now taken care of by a specialised company. There was a luminous label on every trunk capable of transmitting the tree's vital statistics to a distant control centre.

Bobby jumped out of a bush and barked happily when he saw me. Then he launched himself at my calf and I had to shake him off in order to walk.

My aunt hugged me as hard as she could and smiled at me until her cheeks vanished behind her pointy catwoman glasses.

She tried to stay in shape, and sometimes she managed to lose those 15 to 20 years making her seem less decrepit. Compared to my mother Clara, who was actually 8 years younger than her, I reckon Nancy could still make a few old white heads in the park turn around, if only she would ever go there. She even had her groceries delivered fresh to the door every single day.

"Yes aunt, everything's fine."

"No-one bothered you, did they? Terrible things happen even here in Sberbank these days."

"I kept my eyes open."

"Come in, I'll get you something to eat. It's dark already…"

After a quick run through family affairs, about which I knew just enough to still be considered a member, we sat at the dinner table and carried on talking about very different but just as desolate topics:

Permanent economic crisis.

See-sawing political situation.

Unpredictability of the weather in every season.

At least Nancy didn't have the same discouraging expression on her face as her sister. Or the same head-full of bunkum, or the same mouthful of clichés, and especially not that eternal sickly air that depressed me about Clara.

On the contrary, her ruddy cheeks gave her a touch of vitality and likeability.

Aunt Nancy was a parallel world, a next-door universe made up of estuaries of veins, ridiculous clothes, and a completely feminine fragility, ever more worn out by the passing of time. Her top half, straight and prim and proper, was a kind of monument and despite what she had been through, health problems, solitude, old-age and more than anything else her idiot husband, she had decided – in a unilateral manner – to resist all and any centrifugal force and this indomitable attitude made her precious to me. She was my outpost in the city; a fortress I had been able to count on for years.

Nancy was still clearing the table, a smoking cigarette between her fingers, when the doorbell rang.

"I'll go aunt, don't bother yourself."

The entryphone's video showed the image of a kid in a hoody with a shopping trolley behind him.

"90... cents... please."

His voice was hoarse, thick with catarrh, and slowed down by something like chewing-gum. I left the house and when I reached the gate the kid leant forward, resting his hands on the bars of the gate. He was wearing dustman's gloves.

Bobby the useless little pooch growled, but strangely stayed still, keeping at a safe distance.

"Only... 90... cents, please."

Holding out one hand towards me he pulled the other back and stuck it in the shopping trolley's pocket. He was about to brush me with his hand, and that suspicious proximity terrified me.

"No, no...Thank you."

Saying that stupid thing, I threw a kick at Bobby that was standing like a stuffed animal behind me, and then I moved away.

I didn't think that town tramps had come so far yet as to take money straight from your pockets. He was already gone and I went back into the house.

Bobby remained outside, on guard.

"Who was it Roberta?"

"Nobody... I mean there was just this bloke asking for money."

I didn't want to worry her. Knowing that anyone could so easily get their hands on her made me hate my uncle even more.

"At this time of night? Ah, there are too many of them wandering around, at night there's even a curfew. It's not like it used to be any more. Never leave the 'concessions' after sundown."

It sounded like good advice and my drained face perceived it as an embargo. We went to bed after a cup of tea for me and a goodnight shot of rum for my aunt.

After half an hour under the covers I was still awake. Perhaps it was the change of bed, perhaps it was the sound of running water coming from the bathroom. Nancy, just as

I remembered, could spend hours in there, so long that it made me think she wasn't even getting ready to go to bed but for some secret tryst instead. Maybe she'd even found out how to give herself silicone injections. I wondered if my aunt still sometimes had impure dreams even at her age.

For me, putting on makeup was a waste of time, for her it was time well-spent. A little like in economics, where it is the attitude towards time that establishes a nation's success or failure, its financial policies, its ranking in the world register of debtors.

To kill some time I went barefoot into the corridor, took four steps along the purple red carpet and slipped into my aunt's room: a place that had crystallised thirty years ago.

Everything outside her home had transformed so fast as to leave the place without geographical points of reference or economic security, to the point that the Moscova District had become an elegant dormitory for the middle classes and then a residential "banking concession". Nancy's room though had remained the same as ever, the same I remembered from the first time I came in here, crawling.

It had the same '70s wardrobe with the enormous mirror I used to smear with her makeup (at that time I used to like such intense colours). The same straw seated chairs, too high for me to clamber up until I was four. The same bed, with a section of a TAO shape for a headboard which I used to jump off to bounce on the mattress.

The jewellery box was on her mahogany dressing table. I opened it knowing I would find dried flowers, chains, and the costume jewellery Nancy loved making to keep herself busy. There was a letter addressed to my uncle. I decided not to stick my nose any further into that business. Apart from anything else the date was from ten years earlier. Water under the bridge that it wasn't worth running back over.

So I went back into my room, the one Nancy, humouring my fickle eternally unsatisfied nature, had let me change at least about twenty times.

The fact that I slept on a futon mattress just ten centimetres from the floor always left her speechless.

The next day, mid-morning found us sitting eating coffee and cookies; she had even made some of them herself, the only thing she shared with Clara.

"Can I ask you a favour Roberta?"

I nodded as she pulled out some papers from one of the dresser's drawers. It was not a good sign and the paper was covered with rubber stamps and barcodes.

"Last month I got this warning letter. They say I haven't paid my rates. But I've got the receipt, I downloaded it from internet when I paid online. At the Help Desk they say I have to go personally or send an authorised person. Would you mind going for me? You know how these things go."

"No problem, I want to go into town anyway, I can go to the City Council Bank."

"Thanks, you know how I don't really like going out."

I finished eating and got ready to go out. When I was already in the doorway, my aunt sidled up to me, a little timid and a little embarrassed.

"Listen dear... Seeing as you're going out anyway, could you buy me a copy of VOGUE? On the website I saw that this month there are these sweet dress patterns..."

I gave her a hug, careful not to hurt her frail frame. My aunt had not converted to digital magazines for a very simple reason: she could still afford to pay someone to carry on cutting down trees and making paper.

She lit a cigarette, half embarrassed, then waved goodbye to me from the window overlooking the garden.

Outside the 'concessions', Milan was a porous entity: the offices, shops, bars and restaurants dripped one onto the other. Each function integrated with the next, and the effect was disorientating. It was possible to check your emails, and download audio tracks from promotional music clouds anywhere, while drinking a soft drink, trying on virtual clothes, biting into a sandwich, reading the news headlines, analysing the stock exchange ups and downs, or checking the hits of the moment.

You couldn't even tell whether people were working, shopping, or relaxing. Each and every action also included others. Every thought materialised a flow of minute operations on the fragmented surface of behaviour. The words I could hear came from thousands of different slangs, I heard incomprehensible sentences from the mouths of immigrants coming from who knows where... It all looked the same in its diversity, a chaotic background against which I felt so provincial.

Milan fashion, the socio-economic phenomenon that had brought the city immense profits and worldwide fame no longer existed. There was only an infinite variety of ways to dress, clothing hybridism, widespread and permanent, reflecting the general mixture of the people and their styles imported from every corner of the planet.

Outside the 'concessions' the older houses and buildings had been cleared of tenants, or rather some Banking Institute had made them the classic offer they couldn't refuse. This process of delocalisation didn't just concern jobs, in Milan it involved housing too.

The City Council Bank was in Via Monte di Pietà next to the UPIM department store. After an hour of queuing and managing to prove my aunt's innocence to a Help Desk clerk and the immediate cancellation of her debt, I finally started my weekend by watching an improvised show put on by semi-employed actors in the department store's hall.

If they had chosen to perform in this location it meant they attracted more people here than in a theatre. I had even heard about singers who instead of working the usual night-life venues put on shows at motorway toll gates, in post offices, and in hospital wards, or writers who instead of universities and literary cafés preferred holding creative courses in prisons, or even at sports stadiums.

Next to me there was a young man, a kid really, helping an old lady choose clothes. He was explaining to her, index finger raised for emphasis, that of the two garments she could only afford one. The old lady, her eyes swollen with illness or perhaps held back tears, twisted her mouth and dropped a dressing gown back into the 1 euro only basket, holding onto the slippers. The scene struck me and I stood staring at them for a long time, until I left too through the rotating doors of the department store.

As soon as I was out I jumped. A kid wearing the usual hoody with hood up and shopping trolley behind him grabbed my arm.

"Please... nine-ty... cents?"

He was holding onto me and his voice was whining and petulant. The drawled words reminded me of the bloke the other evening by my aunt's gate but it couldn't possibly be the same person. In general I preferred to ignore the idea of meaningful coincidences, although I was certain that they existed: they made me feel impotent, at the mercy of superior forces. For the same reason I hated the "macro-economy" and believed in the healthiness of the "micro-economy", influenced by an infinitely smaller amount of crazy variables.

"No, no... I haven't got any change."

The kid was wearing huge sunglasses that prevented me from seeing his face properly. Catching my reply he spat on the ground, almost as if he were offended, and a droplet of saliva hit my boot. Then he turned away nonchalantly and started dragging his shopping trolley somewhere else.

"You could at least say sorry, you lout!"

As if to put an end to the conversation he stuck his middle finger up at me and hurried off rattling down the street. I was infuriated, I was so mad I started following at a quick march. Despite the biting cold and gusts of dry wind like slaps in the face, I took my hands out of my pockets to help gather speed. I might not be from Milan but that was no reason to consider me less human than the rest of the local population.

He realised I was following him and sped up. He started zigzagging between the parked cars and looked behind him every so often to check if my determination to have a go at him was holding, and how close I was getting.

"Whaddya want? Leave me alone..." he yelled and waved his arms around as if he wanted to scare me off, almost like I had tried with him a little earlier.

"You lout, say you're sorry!"

"Go fuck yourself!"

Instead of scaring me his swearing lit my anger's fuse. My legs moved of their own accord, and I found myself running, with the smell of his worn out coat and trousers covered in filth in my nose. I nearly got him too, my hands reaching for his scrawny neck when at a certain point, following his route with my eyes, I saw the oncoming rubbish lorry.

"Stop, stop now!" I shouted, but he took my warning as a threat, and ignored it.

It was a matter of seconds. As soon as he shot out into the road, the lorry, braking, hit him head on a metre away from me.

The half squashed shopping trolley was transformed into a weapon, like opening one of those Swiss army knives, and once open it let its contents burst out: there was metal in amongst a load of paper, splintered wood and some plastic that was just as hard.

Horrified I stood petrified on the curb, hands in my hair, until I saw a body, floppy and decapitated, appear from under the back wheels.

A group of tramps ran up to it immediately, more to see who the victim was than to attempt to help, given that the head, still wrapped in its hood, had rolled off between two cars. One of them, a mean sneer on his face, pointed determinedly at me, singling me out as the presumed cause. They started debating with each other, muttering in low voices, and after a rapid exchange, they decided to run in my direction.

They thought it was my fault! They thought I had pushed him into the road when in fact I'd tried to warn him.

Another rubbish lorry, without logos on its side this time, pulled up next to the first one, two figures jumped out and gathered up the remains of the dead kid. They lifted him up like he was a sack of rubbish and threw him in the back of the lorry.

Wasn't the poor kid even going to get a decent burial? Didn't they consider him worthy of being treated as a human being?

My throat went dry, and my heart started thumping hard just below my throat.

I ran without thinking about the reasons behind that absurd action.

From that moment everything got a bit confused and in the heat of the chase, trying to get away from my pursuers, I lost my sense of direction.

Rightly thinking that I was escaping from thugs, the people in my path got out of the way and let me through, more to wash their hands of the whole thing and not get involved than anything else. I knew that in the city nobody helped anyone any more, and that everyone – unlike in the country – minded their own business, still I was pleased to see that at least they didn't try to stop my attempts at losing my pursuers.

I know it might sound like a banal commonplace, and it was, because that common place did in fact exist.

I turned into a street, I had no idea which one, and saw an underpass.

I ran into the four-lane tunnel; my pursuers showed no signs of giving up, in fact they had split up and taken two separate roads to reach me better: Two of them were aiming straight for me, while a third was running along the road parallel with me.

Before the end of the tunnel I saw the sign for the train station. The only place crowded enough to lose them in.

There were parked buses waiting to carry travellers to Linate Airport and various police cars were camping out in the depths of the parking area. I took it all in an instant, in one all-encompassing glance. Between knots of people and extra-large suitcases it was hard to make headway.

By this time two of my pursuers were exhausted but the third was less than 5 metres from my noisy boots. His laboured breathing pushed me into making a last effort. I pulled the next day's train ticket out of my coat pocket and slowed down just long enough to justify my hurry in the eyes of the security guard, unworried but on duty at the entrance and blocking my way.

"I'm late, I'm going to miss my train, it's about to go…"

I waved my ticket at him and without even checking the departure time or date he put down his arms and let me through.

The tramp on the other hand ran right into him, his way barred. He shouted and railed at me, yelling that I was a murderer.

I bent over, doubled up, hands resting on my knees trying to get my breath back. Then I turned to look behind me, attempting to somehow communicate my incomprehension at what was happening. Luckily the guard took him to be a crazy and he, feeling taunted, continued to yell and shout, but in the end he had to give up.

I was so happy. Not real happiness, it was that feeling of relief at having escaped from a danger with only a hair's breadth to spare.

In the station, I started looking for somewhere safer, like a waiting room, where I could rest after my flight. It took me a few moments of concentration to bring some calm back to my upset face. I tried calling my aunt but there was no reply. If she was in the bathroom she could be there for hours looking at herself over and over in the mirror, wearing it out at the same time as complaining at every new sign of ageing left on her body.

Finally my breathing was back to normal, and I was sweaty. Sweaty and smelly. I looked around me, intimidated. There were two seedy looking blokes in leather jackets, loitering in front of a kebab shop. Unlike the normal station goers, they appeared to be checking me out attentively. Actually after just a few seconds of scrutiny they ignored me too; the paranoia was officially all my own.

To be on the safe side, I moved further into the waiting room, under the seating sign.

It only was dimly lit, heavy with stale air and there were big piles of boxes stacked in the corners of the room. Lives in boxes containing dreams and desires to send far away, to unknown destinations. A group of oriental tourists was carefully reading an interactive guide about Milan's restaurants and marking places and routes on the virtual map of the city, which they then copied onto their palmtops. Another solitary traveller was sprawled on one of the chairs, heaven knows how long he had been there waiting for a connection to heaven knows where. He had a light reinforced backpack that was so dusty it looked ancient.

I sat on a plastic chair leaving at least three places between me and anyone else, but after a few minutes I felt a stranger's eyes on me. I turned around slowly, at first I saw two hollow cheeks, then the black eyes above them, enormous and magnetic. It was the same kid who had been helping the old lady buy slippers in the UPIM department store. He had a hood up over his head too, his sunglasses though were hanging round his neck on a chain.

Scared by the unpleasant encounter with the tramps earlier, I let him sit next to me anyway without getting unsettled; perhaps unconsciously I wanted to be cheered up, or just protected by someone who I had seen showing a little respect for others.

"Are they looking for you?"

His voice was low and suave. It was strange though, he wasn't looking at me anymore, he was staring at a space directly in front of him.

"How did you know?"

This time he winked and I caught a hint of vanity in his gaze, almost a sense of cunning and that he felt he knew something I didn't.

"I know because we saw you."

I wondered if an eyewitness would have been able to settle the matter of the road accident with the tramps. However, there was still something bothering me. My anxiety was back. Back came the paranoia.

"What do you mean by *we saw you*?"

The bloke turned towards the entrance as the door flew open and a strange crazy looking girl with a blonde bob came towards us. Her nose was quite long and her eyes were green with a wild bird-like look to them.

"Quick, we have to get out of here... They saw her come in. They'll catch all three of us. They've already called more muscle."

The guy grabbed me by the arm. He was urging me to move even though I had absolutely no intention of doing so.

"Wait a moment...what are you talking about? What do you mean muscle?"

He let go of me, but carried on telling me, with eloquent gestures that I should get up and run.

"The bad guys, the guys looking for us. We're running away from them too."

I didn't understand a thing. Either they thought I was someone else or Milan had become such a vortex of chaos that I never wanted to come back here again.

The thought that these two adolescents could clear my name in the eyes of the "baddies" soon left me; in this situation some absurd coincidence had put me in, they could only save me by taking me away from there.

I checked the time on the wall display. Not long now and the dark of evening would be on us. I started running again, with them this time. Once out of the waiting room, we dodged some travellers' belongings and suitcases, slid through the queues outside the ticket office and dashed in between the trolleys and forklifts.

"At least tell me where we're going! I have to get back to Sberbank!"

Golden bob girl turned first. If earlier on she had looked scared, now she seemed happy and exhilarated.

"The first train to leave!"

Then her companion added just as cheerfully and excitedly, "Destination unknown. We do it a lot... C'mon run, hurry up!"

We didn't go anywhere in the end because we were forced to veer away from the platform as soon as my "guides" realised they had been seen by some suspicious characters coming down the tracks. They clearly knew how to recognise their enemies.

"No, no, no... The other way, go the other way, then we'll come back in."

We swerved quickly towards the Bankaiazzo exit. Just outside a battered old pick-up with no roof pulled up and blocked the road in front of us.

Before being able to think up a counter move a hulking man climbed out, his padded jacket made him look even bigger and he grabbed the girl around the waist. Another ugly brute with a beard caught me and my escape companion by our lapels as we tried to clamber over the bonnet of the pick-up. Their faces were stony and impenetrable above broad shoulders.

Struggling was futile. In the excitement of what appeared to be a swift kidnapping, the kid's hood fell to his shoulders, and right there behind a stub of an ear, hidden in the hollow of his neck, I could see the glow of a LED, a blinking light like the one on the dashboard of the car we were being bundled into the back of.

The baddie scrutinised me closely. His toxic breath almost made me sneeze.

"Well well well... a new entry. Well done kids. You managed to convince her, it would have been harder for us."

The girl tried to deny this by shaking her head and got a slap for her pains. She kept her head turned, fingering her cheek.

Then he turned back to me, pressing his thumbs against my cheekbones.

"It's a pleasure to initiate you into a new world; make you lose your virginity... Oh, not physically, of course, I mean spiritually..."

With a malevolent grin he threw us into the back of the pick-up.

"First though, we have to get even with you two skiving truants."

I saw the panic spread in their eyes.

"It's always the same old story. How many times do I have to tell you? You have to come back to base at the end of every bloody shift!"

I was wrong: I had been convinced that bad luck hung over the whole city, but really it was just picking me out for special treatment. Surely it was impossible that they could have mistaken me for one of their own. From the way the baddies acted, there was probably a band of criminals that exploited and abused these kids for their business dealings. Organised begging, petty theft, various illegal acts. Stuff you often saw on TV. I just couldn't believe they had LEDs inserted in their necks so they could be tracked down any time they tried to escape.

The man in the back of the pick-up started smacking the two kids around so violently that they screamed with the blows, they didn't dare complain though for fear of angering their torturer even further.

"Take it easy, don't break them. We still need them in working order!" shouted the driver who appeared to be the "good" one of the pair (by his face he could easily have been the "ugly" one) at his companion.

"Don't worry, I just wanted to discourage their little escape antics. It's all money down the drain."

And he started hitting them with a garden hose he had taken from under a tarpaulin. The hose itself wasn't so painful judging by their reaction, but when the metal nozzle hit them they jumped from one side to the other like insane cats.

"Let's see if this will stop you wanting to run away."

Not satisfied with the treatment he was giving them, he rummaged in a sack and pulled out an axe. He grabbed the girl by her hair and ordered her to take her shoes off.

At first she refused, then when she saw him sharpening the blade against the bodywork of the pick-up with a few sideways blows, she obeyed in tears.

"The sock too, come on. The right foot."

Then he rested the heated metal against the girl's frozen little toe.

I didn't want to watch the amputation so I turned my face the other way, and then I realised that we were stuck in the middle of traffic. Above us I could see the Lima Bank billboard, halfway down Corso Buenos Aires.

With a blow from his other hand the brute pushed the axe hard making it sink into the girl's flesh, cutting clean through the bone. I know because at the last moment, I had to turn and look through the corner of my eye, and I saw the toe roll along the metal bed of the pick-up. The driver started honking the horn like a madman, covering Golden bob girl's screams.

No-one was taking any notice of me, in their hurry they hadn't even tied me up. They were too sure of being able to catch their victims with their tracking system, but I didn't have one of those devices in me, so I jumped out as soon as the car started moving again. If they wanted to hang on to those two poor kids they would have to let me go. Or lose a load of time chasing after all three of us again.

They only noticed I was gone 40 metres further up the road. The boy was waving at me while the baddie swore at me through gritted teeth. Golden-bob girl must have fallen to the floor in pain.

Just to be sure, I left the main road and set off into the side streets. I kept up a fast pace, though I was weighed down by a deep bitterness. I tried calling Nancy again, on the fifth ring she finally picked up.

"Roberta! Where are you? I've been waiting for you for hours."

There were huge mounds of rubbish and heaps of refuse everywhere along the pavements. Enormous murals were a sign that the embers of Milan's youth – whatever genetic hybrid they now had in their DNA – still burned under the ashes of city prohibition notices. That distorted but indomitable form of communication was the proof.

"Yes aunt, I'm lost. I'm trying to get home. Something so weird has happened to me."

In this district the number of insolvent inhabitants must have been very high, so high as to prevent the Lima Bank from being able to afford any kind of street cleaning. It was in that exact moment that I realised the anarchibank system was a system of control. When citizens were transformed into debtors, well and truly harassed, their will bent to the needs of consumerism, they became "good citizens"; taken in by commercial promotions, interested in stock exchange, worried about tariff plans, their whole lives were revolving around economic matters and financial dilemmas without having the smallest actual idea of their causes, and without being able to really understand why. A little like what happens with religion. Spending hidden behind savings, like sin behind prayer. In this way they could keep the mass of consumers in hand, studying their preferences, their favourite brands, their commercial habits and in the space of a short time every single aspect of their behaviour became predictable.

"Where are you right now?"

That question brought me back to my immediate predicament.

There was so little light from the lampposts that the pair of filthy figures with ragged overcoats who jumped out appeared from the shadows as if they had been living in the walls. A nauseating stink preceded them. Behind them were others in even worse condition. Even more came out of the big council bins as if they were city rats. I was overwhelmed by anxiety, my eyes darted all over the place looking for an excuse for my being there. Was I lost? Was I looking for somewhere?

I checked in my pockets to see if the money I had with me might be enough to buy my safety or if there was too little to convince them to leave me alone. Surrounded by those poor wretches panting to get their hands on anything to re-sell or reuse, I could see on their faces the same doubt: is this girl worth stealing from or is she only good for a bit of fun?

To keep talking on the phone with Nancy, pretending to ignore them, was not a good idea. They weren't the type of people I could ask to hold on while I finished talking.

"I don't know aunt! I don't know! I have to leave you now."

By the street signs I was on the corner of Via Lazzaretto and Via Felice Casati, an intestine-like street that appeared to be some sort of trench under siege from people who had ended up talking to themselves or begging change from any passers-by. Perhaps they were the original inhabitants of the district, reduced to living in hardship. All the many dark un-lived-in or abandoned houses might be a valid explanation.

And I was the day's special offer!

Despite the buildings from the early 1900s, the shiny cars and seductive ads, Milan was governed by brutal economic laws; primitive rules of finance where it wasn't even the strongest who survived, but the most adaptable.

One of those moving bodies came closer to me, he was holding a flayed head in his hands. The skull had nails driven into it and instead of a tongue there was the burning stub of a blood-soaked candle.

"I'd like to introduce you to my office manager, when he sacked me I put him in the sack too."

I backed off from that macabre sight and heard a sound like frying insects, the same sound as those things that protect you from mosquito bites in the summer. Then I noticed the image that had been pursuing me since I had got to the city: the same "ninety cents" kid, wearing a hoody with the hood up was coming up to me with the same shopping trolley pulled behind him. His hand held out in front of him as if begging, his cadaverous face hidden by sunglasses even in the night time, in the middle of winter.

He moved along right up against the wall, like a spider: not one of those that spin thickly woven webs of fine threads to capture their prey, but an arachnid with speed and strength, one that attacks directly. A spider from a documentary.

He grabbed my arm and his words were no surprise, they were the same words that in just a few hours I had come to know only too well. I was scared that even the hair on his face might sting like that of some spiders.

"Nine-ty cents, please..."

I didn't give him the time to do anything else, I wriggled away and hurried off fast.

Him and his damned pointy hood! I saw them everywhere!

The rest of the siege party didn't bother to follow me. Most of them were old couples, a bunch of decrepit pensioners whose joints struggled just to keep them standing. They wobbled a little towards me, held up by the hope of following the begging operation through to a beneficial end, then they gave up, preferring to rummage around in the depths of the council bins.

Along Viale Tunisia I finally had time to think things over: it hadn't been the kids who chased me but their bosses who, for some reason, wanted me too. Not out of malevolence, but the pure and simple need for labour.

Those kids were a "derivative" of the anarchibank system.

High above Milan there were no stars to be seen in the pale orange sky and off the top of my head I couldn't think of any other way of getting my bearings. Attempting to stop someone was old fashioned, frowned on, and almost illegal. The risk of being ignored was little greater than, in the best-case scenario, being insulted and sworn at.

For decades, the other Italian regions had continued to send men and women to Milan, and Milan carried on receiving a portion of them. The rest ended up being sent back, some having made their fortunes, some without a penny, but all of them deprived of their illusions.

The anarchibank regime had ripped the veil from the stage of affairs: removed the curtains from the bankruptcy policies and uncovered the thousands of financial tricks with which State and employees were liquidated, the system wasn't even a social slaughterhouse, it was a complete madhouse.

Finally, after turning into street after street that all looked the same, I recognised the silhouette of Porta Venezia's Ramparts. I knew where I was and I knew that if I went along the avenue until I got to the Porta Volta Bank I would be able to find my way home.

A few street lamps with bulbs that had survived the vandals lighted my way. The ramparts accompanied me up to Porta Nuova along a straight stretch of road with racing cars and anxious pedestrians going just as fast. The only shops open were the night fast food take-aways and the consumer credit "Kwik-fix-loans" micro-credit franchises.

In all that confusion, between being chased, witnessing mutilation and other everyday horrors created by the economic madness Milan had been overwhelmed by, I realised I hadn't bought Nancy her magazine, nor was I in the mood to go back now to do so.

When I finally got to the gate of aunt Nancy's house, she was mounting the guard under the porch, holding Bobby, that useless old bag of fleas, in her arms as if she were levelling a rifle.

I didn't tell her much; in fact I excused myself and asked if she minded if I went straight to bed after all the nasty surprises of the day. Nancy was understanding and saved me from the pain of explaining everything that had happened. We women understand some things from each other's silences.

Under the covers I tried with all my might to sleep, instead the images of the day's terrifying and shocking encounters kept running through my head.

They didn't let up for hours and hours: "nine-ty cents" echoed around my head with the same cadence as a death bell tolling, even though, when I came to think about it, that plea had always been expressed in a subdued and pitiful manner, never aggressively.

What had happened to those two kids? What train would they jump on at their first opportunity?

When I finally managed to fall asleep, it gave no relief to my state of mind; I dreamed of a snail, a long viscid slug I was attempting to push out of my mouth, a feat requiring an inhuman effort. My lips pulled back unnaturally, my jaw gave way and was left hanging from my face, long and disfigured.

This scene lasted all night, worse than giving birth.

I woke up and was rubbing my jaw when I heard someone ringing on the entryphone. A wave of fear hit me. Fear of the tramps, fear of yesterday's bosses. I threw on a jumper, worried about aunt Nancy on her own at the gate, and ran downstairs as fast as I could.

She was already in the garden, shivering in her kimono dressing-gown by the gate. I heard that odious line again: "nine-ty cents please."

Nancy put her hand in a pocket and then held it out through the bars and... paid for her *newspaper*. The kid who at night had looked to me like a beggar, in the daylight turned out to be the newspaper boy? A door to door newsagent?

The kid moved away furtively while Nancy turned towards me, her eyes were swollen with tears.

"Those poor kids. Children can't even leave their houses alone without risking being kidnapped by some concessions gang to end up just like them."

Her eyelids were wrinkled and rough, and her lips ruched in vertical lines like an old rubber band. She rolled up her newspaper vigorously and slipped her arm through mine.

"The least fortunate are set to begging, the others help old people and offer small services for money."

As we crossed the garden, Nancy scratched her head, then sniffed her nails. The smell of the paper irritated her. It wasn't the same paper as the Vogue magazine. Yet, you could shake and try to rock her, but she always stayed unshaken and impassive, like water in a leaning bottle.

"I saw them close up yesterday, Nancy. Those kids have LEDs in their necks, even if they try to run away they get caught again."

She sighed, hunted for a cigarette in her dressing-gown pockets, and lit up.

"Yes I know. They don't talk about it on TV but I see them here at the gate every day. Nobody wants to believe in certain ghosts. They prefer to entertain themselves with the make-believe ones."

We went back into the house and my aunt threw the paper on the table.

"Wait here. I'll be right back."

After a few seconds she came down the stairs with a big embroidered box: her beloved jewellery case.

Inside, as well as the chains I had seen the previous evening, there was a collection of dried flowers. Little roses to be exact, lots of different coloured little roses. She had collected them such a long time ago that there was a thick layer of grey dust on the petals.

"Those kids are like these flowers, they never really wither, even though they have been dried out."

She held out the box to me. In general, I didn't have much faith in words, and she could read that in my expression.

"They are not actually either alive or dead, Roberta."

I waited, I got the feeling she was about to let me into a secret, but she said no more. Sometimes aunt Nancy would come out with these things, mournful observations about how time had stolen something beautiful from her flowers, something only they had possessed and that had vanished. This is why she kept them.

Seeing them like this, in their decrepit beauty, made me believe that she might be right. Is this why aunt Nancy bought her newspapers from the door to door newsagents?

"Read the letter."

The one I hadn't wanted to open.

I took the envelope with my uncle's name written in block letters and opened it warily. Actually there was no letter to my uncle in the envelope, instead there was a long list of product codes, a concise description, followed by the price. It was an invoice dated eight years before, an invoice for technological equipment. The highest sum was for Light Emitting Diodes, 500,000 pieces, sent to my uncle's address in Milan before he moved his residence to China.

In the afternoon, when I was back on the Intercity train staring out of the carriage window, I thought that being unknowing and perhaps blissful ignorance were really a state of grace. It was a rare thing to be allowed to stay in that permanent state of ignorance, of pure innocence. I was on my way back home to my town, yet in that instant and with that same movement, the knowledge of what I had experienced in Milan had taken me forwards. Part of me was confused. Immersed in the silence of the train, forehead resting against the glass, I wanted to be comforted by Clara, even though I no longer felt the need for her personal "vitamins".

After that, I saw other ghosts away from the TV screens, but they no longer scared me so much. Strangely, that train could have taken me to any destination.

FLUSH

translation by Georgia Emma Gili

When I tried it the first time, I didn't know what to expect. Disappearing, maybe dying and then reappearing, but where and, above all, *as what*?

No-one knew anything about it. Or rather, no-one talked about it without losing track of themselves in grumblings and stumblings. Including those who swore they had survived the most terrifying experience of their life. From the faces they were making they passed it off as conclusive proof: they were stronger because they were still alive.

So why did I want to do it? Why did I want to subject myself to such torture?

I check the time, then the club sign and say to myself: Simon, are you sure it's worth it?

The *trance* music making the blood pump in your veins follows its own beat at 150 bpm. It rebounds outside, along the chipped walls of the alleyway dripping with humidity and fluorescent paints.

Some shady figures are haggling in the shadows. Everything is competing to distract me.

My clothing is unlikely: beige trousers from when I weighed 90 kilos, a light blue shirt which I didn't know I had, and some old, brown, inveterate tourist sandals.

I switch off my smartphone so as not to be wed to some overly invasive urban application.

The place where I have the appointment, the Lair of the White Noise, is not an establishment that you would want

95

to attract attention in. It's a suburb club haunted by ear-splitting volume fanatics, with the type of din which distracts you and can make you change your mind every three minutes. Even less, if you're with someone who'll be your sound box.

Maybe that's why I made up my mind. To drop myself into the "well" and slip into the Lair of Noise. Not very differently from those who had dropped in beforehand and would have done so afterwards.

From outside, the Lair looks worse than a hole dug in the ground. The entrance is a leaning metal sheet attached to thick hinges sunk into stone. Beyond that, you plunge into a tunnel lit only by oblique candle lights. The air is moved both by the vibrations of the music and by the large air ducts.

In one wide stretch, a dusty cave serves as a dance floor and around it are set out some nailed boards, painted red. Wallowing in a ripped VIRGIN AIRLINES seat is an olive-skinned guy in a paramilitary jumpsuit.

I approach him with a nod and he offers me a crooked smile and a jeweller's shop set of teeth.

My contact, Charlie Four Fingers, had been a good go-between. Maybe he had asked his girlfriend to perform a *lap-a-samba* for the bloke. Maybe she had been good at making him forget a wretched day. As a matter of fact, Tony has agreed to meet me. He lifts a bony hand and beckons me to follow him.

"In the toilets. In a minute. I go in first."

But he doesn't say anything else. Is there a right way of doing this? Are there any precautions to follow? What should you avoid to keep yourself out of harm's way?

I've eaten a *spring roll* and drunk two beers. Maybe I should wait. Or maybe I'm hesitating because I'm not convinced.

In spite of things, I've let myself be influenced by the voices going round, those on the air that turns into strings in your head, black holes in your understanding and vortices of alienation.

Absurd voices that talk of decompression voids in your soul, and mirror-thoughts from the memories of others. Mental boxes inside other boxes.

Illusions so unpleasant and disturbing as to make you lose your sense of direction and lucidity. Shit, how many versions of the same thing exist?

Okay, it's a subjective fact, something that all of us live by *ourselves* and *for ourselves*, but surely there must be a common denominator, something which can only be associated with the phenomenon of the *Flush*.

The Flush or the Whirlpool is the experience in question's *nom de guerre*: The Silencer, on the other hand, is the name which half the authorities around the planet have used to ban it.

Nothing remains but for me to discover the reason for this choice of name.

I breathe in and start walking towards the flashing toilet symbol.

To reach it I have to keep an eye out for those getting off to the rhythm of a beat interspliced with cannon booms.

If they call them "schizophonics", there's a reason...

I've never sniffed happy dust in all my life. Skunk spliffs and *hash* cakes, some glue fumes and at the very most some subliminal dosers. But I've never touched coke, "*h*", mescaline, amphetamines or LSD. I like communing with nature, so to speak. And yet, for the Flush I'm ready to break this rule.

Whatever it was, this experience would circulate inside me, it would flow in my veins or into any other organ it could spread to.

I cross the threshold of the bathroom after having exited the acoustic treatment of the dance floor unscathed.

My ears are whistling and regurgitate excess peaks of melody. Inside, I'm stunned by the thunderous noise from all the taps running, vomiting up a thick, greenish liquid. What they had taught us to use with caution since we were kids: that greenish fluid, with a vaguely minty smell (no-one is able to tell you the taste without copping a stomach pump) is to be blamed on the chemical agent used to exterminate any noxious substances.

If they call it "preventive hygiene", there's a reason…

Lying in wait, behind the door like a feline, Tony swiftly hangs a sign outside saying OUT OF ORDER and then locks us in. I have almost two minutes before the hunt for a free urinal kicks off.

"Are you Simon?"

"Yes, that's me, Four Fingers' friend."

I go to take out an identity card, but he blocks me.

"I'll take your word for it. In any case, I need to see the money first."

"Wait, I want to try it out. How do I know you're not fobbing me off with some low frequency crap."

The bloke knits his brows: if I'm coming out with bollocks like that it means it's my *first time*. And so he starts to treat me like a junkie, like any old schizophonic, greedy for novelties to get off on.

"You'll have to trust me, mate. I can't let you sample this stuff."

I shut up. The mystery of the Flush has tricked me at its outset. Nothing remains but to open my hand and offer him the agreed payment.

He reaches out his arm and takes my credits.

Then he smiles sardonically and opens the other cupped hand.

"Have fun and keep shtum. If they catch you, swallow them. They're biodegradable. They won't show up in a faeces tests. They'd have to open up your stomach within half an hour to nail you."

That said, Tony leaps Siamese-cat style onto the basin and slides through the opening in the top window. He never uses the same door twice.

Before he disappears off into the alleyway, he hisses towards me.

"Mate, take the sign down if you don't want them to smash the door to smithereens for starters and then you."

For a second I'm frozen, doubtful about having lightened myself of a few credits for nothing. Then I lower my gaze to my palm and see what I've bought for the equivalent of two months' rent.

A pair of fucking earphones? Two paltry earplugs?

I can't believe it. They dare to raise these lowly contrivances to the rank of synthetic drug? I flip them over in my hand, intent on digging out a deeper meaning, when threatening blows against the door wake me from the hypnosis of a rip off. I stick the earphones in my pocket and run out dodging a couple of wild men whose bursting bladders are the cause of my salvation.

Simple bitchin' in my direction won't hurt me very much. I go back through the tunnel, this time upwards. I pant and gasp for breath.

The smoke blocks my sight and ravages my sense of smell, the incessant noise makes mincemeat of what's left. I shake my head trying to get a grip. Even just an arm hold to guide me back out. I stagger and reel from one shoulder to the next. Banging into strangers who scoff or round on me angrily.

I count the number of turns and fix my eyes on the walls to make out where I am. The air shakes and rumbles with the echoes of a bass that cuts through your flesh, crackles in your ears, gets absorbed and is only partly deadened.

I catch sight of the emergency strip lighting in the distance. It has to show the way to the surface.

I have double vision and blood is trickling from my ears. It feels white hot like the sound frequency. I grab a rail, there, where every night countless people pass out.

Outside the Lair of the White Noise, I get my breath back.

In the midst of the muffled sounds in the alleyway, with blinded eyes and anaesthetized ears, I am tempted to try the Flush effect, right there and then.

I clock two din-armed geezers and three sylphs in a groupette protected by an aura of defensive music. So, I give up on the idea. I wouldn't want them to attack me with some unknown sound.

Yet, thinking about it, what could happen to me that could be so horrendous if even plain old earplugs are on the drug blacklist?

I think back to Tony who, at this point, must be knocking back a drink in my name.

With the earplugs in my pocket, I start walking stealthily, with bated breath. I turn into Columbus Avenue and while, on the one hand, the Doppler effect, emitted by the high-powered muscle cars doesn't bother me very much, on the other, it's a nuisance: I'm carrying illegal stuff and anyone could get out of a car, point a "double-bad sound" at me and force me to undergo an on-the-spot body search.

The pavement, in the stretch of highway where they've unveiled a 24x7 HyperStore, is teeming with *nocturnals*, young and not so young people, with easy banter and One-Man-Sound intent on selling insults and exchangeable pick-up lines.

Right now, my ears hurt all the time if I don't wear my Sennheiser padded headphones to isolate me from sounds, using other sounds. I was fool to leave them at home. Sounds to drive away sounds: if they call it "low-satisfaction therapy", there's a reason...

I look around for a quiet spot, a park, a garage or any other disused place where a truce could be offered, even momentarily, from the relentlessness noise, from the spirals which are clogging up my ears.

After all, we all want to escape. Those who escape into the TV, or by shopping, or at football stadiums or clubs. And no-one wants to be anywhere else at *that* moment in time.

Those who shut themselves off inside apparent escape mechanisms are simply acknowledging illusory flights from reality. Prisons inside other prisons. Sounds inside other sounds. With only a worsening effect over time.

Those who really flee don't come back. They don't change channel, or go looking for an alternative shop. They don't change political party, or join the latest club. Those in flight aren't really looking for something, they've already *found* it.

My soundproof barrier, made out of two lobe-shaped prongs of my ears, has stopped oscillating. It's my dowser's way of finding the X-spot, where sounds can't reach me or entangle me in a web of distractions.

Where I am, there's no need to make a commotion to be heard. I glance back in both directions.

The seesawing breeze between the isolated branches continues to require the smallest fraction of my attention.

To compensate, the nearest human being is at least 100 yards away. Such a gap as to reassure me and nudge me into getting the earplugs out of my pocket.

I set myself down on a bench along the tree-lined path. In full control of the neighbourhood sound-spectrum, I look at the day's purchases: long, cone-shaped, in a skin-camouflage tone. They're covered in a spongy material that I don't recognise. They're not made of plastic or cork or rubber.

Who knows how the molecules that surround us are shaken in the everyday items that we use?

The more I look at them, the more they seem alien to me, pervaded with a mix of anger about Tony's prohibitively rip-off pricing and curiosity towards an object that, at least in theory, promises to give me a unique experience in return.

I shake them to and fro.

The discussion forums that I took part in before coming to a decision didn't give any advice or tips. Maybe there aren't any. Maybe it's a question of instinct.

Then, I run into an obvious fact: such simple objects can't possibly transmit such complex experiences. So I separate the earplugs, and hold them up at eye level. I observe the cones pointing at each other, ideally.

In the middle, I'm the one keeping the circuit open. Which is what prompts me. I understand the mystery, but I daren't make the leap.

Slowly as a monk preparing tea, I bring the earplugs up to my ears. I look right, then left. I can't understand if I'm putting myself between them or if they're working through me.

In unison, I bring my hands near to one another and let the ambiguous consistency of the wedge-shaped material slip into my ear canal and mould itself to the shape of my eardrum.

It is a rarefied tactile sensation, even perceptible in the obscurity of the skin within my ear.

After having softly pushed in the two ends, I am unaware of *going down*. I'm in the middle of a frown, when I instinctively feel the presence of another reality: *total silence*. Almost accommodating this state, I half-close my eyes.

Silence together with pitch black should be taken in very small doses. Infinitesimally small doses.

Shit, if in historical terms, getting off your head has always been connected to some kind of distortion, a pleasing deformation of reality, then I've started on some serious substance abuse.

It's like a pressure drop on a plane, a sense of suction which first lengthens and then compresses you.

It's absurd, despite being true, the image of air turning into strings in your head, a rarefied space, vacuous and sidereal where my brain used to be.

The absence of auditory perceptions, in contrast with noise permeating everything, works subtly from inside: absolute silence is too dizzying and opens up chasms inside itself, ripping apart any false sense of self-control.

At first, alert and aware of where I am, I imagine how increasing doses of the *Flush* lead to undiscovered places, chasms of self that are normally inaccessible to consciousness, bombarded by sounds.

Then, panic.

A *voided-mind*, free from even the smallest undulation and distraction, what advanced users prattle and moan about on the sites dedicated to this phenomenon, opens up its path *within* me.

My murkiest fears and most remote hopes are condensed onto a visual which is as real as it is dreamable.

Cirrus form visions of my ex-girlfriends form in layers under clouds pregnant with fear and anxiety. In the midst of this, sharp flashes spark off memories.

In the silence of muffled reality, what takes shape can't be controlled, or moulded into any gradation.

The office where I work as an IT specialist is no longer the deafening open-plan room where privacy is knowingly violated, but seems to be a beehive, inhabited by drones who play the part of the victim to business queens bordering on working-time hysteria.

My very own Elisa turns into a vulgar ebony pillar, a Doric column of hard-core scenes, taken and thrown onto flesh as the vessel of my own personal Kamasutra.

Maybe dreaming is the closest paragon to what I'm living. An hallucinatory thread, lucid and yet blurred, a virulent disorientation whose inconsistency is guided to the smallest degree by the active mind.

The concepts which I measure my identity against and which I recognise myself in are sliding away, scared off by the uncomfortable presence of such a unique and rare event.

In terms of anatomy, history and culture, as we are human beings, we are all linked to physical communication, what's written and spoken. Even when dumb panic takes hold, and silence persists inside us for a longish stretch of time, consciousness is switched on.

Not even the accelerated but constant beat of my heart comforts me. I possess an existence beyond mental fluctuations, but nevertheless, I am in freefall.

Using extraordinary willpower, I open my eyes and surprise! A world as mute as I am reveals its silent face to me.

Leaves rustle between the branches, birds sail through the skies in orderly flocks, and the crickets sing in the grass, driven by a breath of wind.

Everywhere there is irreparable quiet and silence.

A veil has been thrown over the sound side of reality, a slap of reality stings me in the face. How many parts of my brain are taken hostage by sound? How much of us is lost in paying attention to it?

I would never want to be deaf, even if a prosthesis can fully restore the joy of hearing, special effects included, still I can understand why the Flush is illegal.

The monotony of the absence of sound is a switch which can be flicked to get high on and at the same time is definitive, demonstrative proof of having survived yourself.

Two facts which, if kept apart, can be accused of degenerating the spirit and spreading practices which harm personal safety and wellbeing, but which, if put together in a single, unique moment, reinforce the ability to focus on and free yourself from the shackles of distraction.

The risk is of a PVS (Persistent Vegetative State) and the incommunicability of a silence where each of us is an island in a sea of emotions, so fluid, insubstantial and malleable as to repudiate words. But even these are impediments which can be overcome by diffusing the shared ritual of the Flush: bands of *silenced* youths can already be seen going around absorbed in contemplating a higher existence, immune to the entrapment of shiny shop windows, hymns to consumerism, and a flood of sublime subliminal signals.

They gesture, moving their hands in the complex grammatical manoeuvres of LSD, the Language of Signs for the Devocalised, and wave their arms about in a mime all of their own, inaccessible to others.

Stripped of every sound-coating, I get up and wander along the dumb, eloquent paths in *another way*. With a tongue which is free from all discord, communicating more intense forms of truth, senses renewed at the root.

It's a premonition...

It puts what's below the hearing threshold into focus.

What strikes me is that I'm *out of tune*.

translation by Michael Colbert

"There it is! Down there! Land!" Billai yelled, nearly fall-ing off the dinghy.

We all looked in the direction she indicated with her arm. The waves that had shaken us for some hundred hours didn't jolt us as much as her words.

We couldn't feel our legs or move a muscle. Tangled one on top of the other, we were groggy from hunger and thirst. Muna, seated next to me, hugged her baby closer. The three guys in front exchanged a hopeful smile. Meanwhile Haz-iz—who came to Bengasi after crossing the Bamako Desert—shook his hand.

"It can't be Italy. We're still far."

We looked at each other anxiously. Someone had fainted. To revive him, we had to slap his face. It wasn't a boat that we had navigated in but a coffin.

"He's right," said Professor Kysmayo, the ex-radio host from Nairobi. "The outline is too simple. It's not the coast..."

Nobody said anything else, because nobody dared pro-nounce the name that, for some weeks, was circulating the Mediterranean's southern shores.

A dark and continuous line occupied the horizon from Otranto in Italy, arriving in Orikum in Albania. Smooth and unassailable, the bulkheads of the naval blockade rose for thirty meters on the sea waves; assembled easily thanks to the ships' containers full of carbon, but impossible to climb or break down, they represented a momentary solu-tion (even though there were those who would've called it the "definitive deterrent") to immigration towards Europe by the sea.

"They said this part was free!" Billai shouted.

"They lied," Haziz said, almost in a whisper.

"Maybe not...I heard barriers can be 3D-printed overnight. The same bulkheads could've been between Pantelleria, Lampedusa and Malta...to force boats to turn around or follow long and expensive routes," Professor Kysmayo said.

Billai rubbed her temples with her fingers. Every border depressed her, and getting closer to a wall, erected for the sole purpose of separating international and domestic waters, discouraged her even further. With her life savings, she had crossed with me the borders of Kenya, Sudan and Libya before attempting the Benghazi crossing.

"Why didn't they tell us?" Muna said.

Nobody felt like answering such a naive question.

"They want to canalize boats to navigable checkpoints," the professor said. "And then come those..." he concluded, pointing to a spot in the distance.

Some black spots, which from far away looked like seagulls, revealed themselves to be surveillance drones activated by the boat's movement detected by satellite. I'd heard about those and others used in the mountains to secure Europe's land borders. Soon, they circled over us like vultures.

With a solemn air, as if she were about to declare war on the world, Billai rose to her feet. Swaying, she grasped my back so as not to fall and said, "We've all lived through things that we shouldn't have lived through and would be better to forget. I'm not turning back. Those drones are informing someone. They'll come and take us. Doctors without Borders, NGOs, the Coast Guard..."

Four hours later, one hundred and thirty-two of us were saved.

I was seventeen years old and my life was contained in a backpack: a bar of soap, a smartphone and charger, a sports jersey (number ten, Ike Kamau), and a photo of my mom and brother. They always told me that I had a narrow head, pointed chin, and quick eyes, black like tar. Like my dad's.

I was seventeen years old and my life had been spent in a refugee camp; since when we arrived in Dadaab from Nairobi, I hadn't seen anything but tents, dust, fences, and gates.

Soft clouds glided over the sea: that night the stars would disappear and the moon would have illuminated us all if another silhouette hadn't appeared to divert the way of our gazes and our lives.

"That's an....aircraft carrier?" Billai asked.

An immense structure stood out on the dark waters.

"I don't know," I said while she drew near me. The lapping of the water had worn down her combative temperament.

Someone took a picture, but in the high seas there wasn't a strong enough signal to transform anxiety into hope. It could be a military ship charged with bringing us back to the dark side of the Mediterranean, but instead the man who drew near us on a lifeboat with four sailors told us a different story.

"Welcome," he said in English. He had blond hair tied back in a ponytail, a pronounced nose and lips, and a smile, sincere but strained. "My name is Sergio Torriani and that's a Green Ship," he added, pointing behind him. "We take in anybody who needs help."

The sailors threw us water bottles.

Haziz grabbed my sleeve and asked me to translate. I was one of the few on board, along with Professor Kysmayo, who knew some English besides Swahili. When I was little, I listened to his show "Indie Reggae, Beats & Rock" on Radio Kenyamoja.com, and I knew hundreds of songs by heart.

"We don't want to board. We want Europe," I said dryly, gesturing to Haziz to show Sergio who those words came from.

He didn't answer right away but instead tossed us a line that Billai caught in the air. "Europe doesn't want you," he continued, bitter, "and they don't care if you're escaping from hunger or war, if you live in refugee camps or if your children and grandchildren will be born and grow up in those prisons. Where do you come from?"

I heard the names of camps I knew like Dadaab, Nyarugusu, Bokolmanyo and others I didn't know like Urfa, Zaatri and Adiharush.

"Besides, this isn't a boat for transit," Sergio said.

"So you'll bring us back or send us to a center for identification and deportation." I translated for Muna, who'd lifted the bundle with her son inside.

"No deportation. The Green Ship is a humanitarian project for the rescue of political refugees and climate migrants."

"If you're not bringing us back and you're not going to Europe, where are you going?" Professor Kysmayo asked. He was the only one to reason with his head and not his heart.

Sergio and the other sailors were already throwing lines to ease the transfer onto their lifeboat.

"Board and you'll see."

Once we'd boarded, Sergio asked, "Nobody else?"

We looked at each other without the courage to respond. Then Professor Kysmayo said, "In the hold there were two cadavers. They died two days ago. They started to stink. We had to leave them at sea...to lighten our load."

"Their names?"

We were silent. Sergio added two Xs to the list of one hundred twenty-three.

From the parapet, I observed the wake of boats in transit in the Aegean Sea: a Greek ferry, two cargo boats, a cruise ship. Who knew how many immigrants were hidden like cargo in the holds.

The others were still sleeping among the trees, and they were not alone: hundreds of strangers were camping in sleeping bags and tents, and below, thousands were squished in the bunks. Yesterday evening, I didn't see anything because I quickly lay down to rest, but now, by the light of dawn, things appeared more clearly.

"Jambo," Sergio said in Swahili, offering me a cup of coffee.

"Jambo, and thank you for picking us up," I said, taking a sip.

"Did you sleep? It's not easy after being on a dinghy."

He must have had experience with migrants to speak like that.

"Little and poorly."

"Later we'll have a soccer game with everyone. Would you want to join?"

I nodded a yes and he convinced me to tell him about "our" games in Nairobi.

"Two things were important for me: surviving and playing soccer...then it became only one when men from al-Shabaab came to the fields where my brother Noor and I played. They scolded us because we wore shorts and played with a ball. Soccer was a decadent pastime for them...like alcohol, cigarettes or film. But Noor and I played it just the same, hidden. Our games ended when the bombs dropped."

I took the Ike Kamau jersey from my backpack.

"Here you can play without anyone saying anything to you."

I gave him the empty coffee cup. "This ship is really odd."

It was his turn to tell me something.

"According to international law, it's not a ship, but a micronation. First it was a bioconservation project funded by the United Nations, a bit like the seed deposits in the Norwegian Svalbaard Islands. Ever heard of it?"

I shook my head.

"Then it was converted to manage the immigrant crisis in the Mediterranean."

Three hills, in the middle of which ran a stream, recreated microclimates: temperate, desert, and Mediterranean. My gaze wandered to the Mediterranean habitat where tens of drones hurried around like birds that watered leaves, cut branches, checked flowers, and collected pollen, while some gardeners oversaw the operations to maintain everything green. Then, in the middle of the eucalyptus grove, I saw an impressive sequoia, its fronds shading half of the ship.

"The habitats," Sergio continued, "are protected by geodetic cupolas one-hundred fifty meters tall. Fresh water comes from a desalinator powered by solar energy."

In the meantime, Billai had woken up and joined us.

"How did you manage to create...all of this?" she asked as if she'd woken into a dream. While I translated, Sergio showed us along a path.

Professor Kysmayo noticed us and joined up. His background as a radio journalist got the better of his sleepiness. When he wasn't on the air with "Indie Reggae, Beats and Rock," he edited a feature on technology.

"We bought an abandoned aircraft carrier, and we modified it through a crowdfunding project. The hull belonged to *Variago*, an aircraft carrier in the same class as Admiral

Kutnetzov launched in 1988 in Russia. In 2004 it was re-baptized *Liaoning* and sold to China to become a floating theme park, like Disneyland, but luckily it didn't happen. We bought it for a token price to make a botanical garden. Ours is a scientific project approved by the United Nations, though now we're more like public transit for migrants," Sergio said with a laugh.

The ship flew its own flag: a sequoia styled green on a hull over a white background.

"We can host seven thousand people. We grow crops and raise livestock. We have internet and 3D printers for any needs."

"Do you want to bring all refugees aboard?" I asked, jokingly. "Like Noah's ark?"

"Impossible. You'd need a hundred ships," Billai added, "and only to evacuate the camp in Dadaab."

"In fact, we have another plan. When the time is right, we'll head towards India and the southern seas."

"Somebody won't like that solution," Kysmayo said.

Haziz and some other guys had boarded reluctantly. They'd continued to complain about wanting only Europe.

"Once they feel better, they have to decide whether or not to retry their journey. We had to save them and let them know the risks."

Streaks of lightning invaded the northern sky. From the Indian hinterlands the cloudy front advanced slowly, like a wounded animal with its head swaying. The weather warped ahead, rumbling and hiding every ray of sun. Lights descended on the water after flashing along incandescent segments.

Many of us retreated to the tents to safely enjoy this spectacle of light, water, and wind while others ran through the torrential rain to refresh themselves in song and laughter.

Muna played with her son, alive thanks to the fact that he'd never been removed from his mother's breast, from which he managed to suck every drop of milk she managed to produce without dying from dehydration.

But the celebrations were interrupted when a man came down from the bridge with a megaphone in hand.

"Attention! Attention! They've detected a seaquake. Time of impact is four minutes."

A sinister light whitened the sea. Billai curled into me.

"It'll never end...even the sea has it in for us."

"Would you have preferred to do as Haziz and his friends did?"

"No, they're crazy to return to Somalia and retry that hopeless journey. But what end will we meet?"

"They say they wanted to retry, but their eyes said otherwise. We'll meet a better end. I'm sure of it."

In the middle of rolling waves four meters tall that battled the ship's hull, another one appeared: it occupied all of the horizon, and judging by the distance, it must've been three times as high. Visibility lowered and a wall of water, misty with the gusts of wind, rustled the branches of the floating forest.

The pitch, already agitated every time the ship sank into the gulch of the waves, became insupportable. Songs and screams became complaints and curses. Those who danced before now grasped onto something, trying not to vomit.

The clamor escalated, an uproar of wind, pounding of water, a vibration like a drumroll beating the charge. Despite the five hundred meter length and its scary tonnage, even the Green Ship suffered from the force of nature.

When the tsunami washed over us, into every pore, nerve, and muscle of our bodies, Billai, her lips trembling with fear and emotion, kissed me on the lips.

Once the storm ended, lights appeared on the horizon.

When we were closer, I made out numerous boats linked together by a series of ropes and jetties: together they all formed a type of flotilla.

None of us had any idea where we'd arrived, even though that assembly in the high sea didn't seem to be our final destination. To find an answer, I went to Sergio, who was on the phone.

"Where and when did it happen?" he was asking someone. A contagious joy appeared on his face, as if he just discovered that he'd become a father.

"And how big is it?"

He walked back and forth, unable to contain his mysterious happiness.

"Yes, definitely...send me a scan and the coordinates. I'll inform the flotilla."

Once he hung up, Sergio grabbed me by the shoulders.

"We've been blessed. Nature is building your new home."

"A new home?"

"The seaquake...it opened a fault line under the ocean from which magma is pumping out."

"Are you bringing us into a volcano?"

"No, but as soon as the magma cools, we can claim the island that's emerging from the sea. Now we too have something to teach Nature. Then with the flotilla we'll think of the rest."

"The rest? That's just going to be a rock."

"Yes, at first it'll be uninhabitable, but we'll terraform it."

I turned my gaze from Sergio's satisfied face to the geodetic cupolas. Tree pollen and mushroom spores floated around, carried by the ocean breeze.

The Green Ship took the lead of the flotilla. Seen from above, it might look like a school of fish migrating for the season. And we were part of that flow.

The sign posted on top of our new land had been modified. By changing an N into a D, it was transformed from "No Man's land" to "No-Mad Land," as the media had hastened to rebaptize the newly born micronation.

The islet where Sergio had first planted the flag–in his haste called "No Man's Land" to underline its independence from whoever wanted to claim the territory–in time became "No-Mad Land" for us. A place accessible without a passport, entry visa, or residency permit. A land designed to welcome people instead of turning them away.

I liked the wordplay of No-Man and No-Mad. Having grown up in a refugee camp between walls and gates, I'd been freed of those limits and I'd left all borders behind. Because borders, political or mental, are temporary obstacles. Because only those who have been turned away or who have enough imagination and empathy for others know how to appreciate the value of hospitality.

The accidental but highly probable birth of the islet in the middle of the Indian Ocean was followed by a phase of movement of thousands of tons of sand from the adjacent seafloor. Thanks to pumping systems, the aspirated sand provided construction material for five enormous 3D printers.

Two of them, aboard tankers, employed the same techniques that the Dutch used to tear the polders from the North Sea–creating dykes of natural material–to protect the central atoll. Yet, different from the polder, the architects supporting the project had thought up a porous, artificial structure that, adequate to host marine life, over the course of centuries would in part replace the irremediably damaged Great Barrier Reef.

The other printers focused on terraforming the cooling magma, rich with fertile substances. They mixed it with sand from the seafloor.

It took us six months before we could set foot on "No-Mad Land."

To our touch, the ground was not hard, but instead it seemed fat and ready to be cultivated.

Under an orange sky, a carpet of yellow narcissus welcomed Billai and me. The air smelled fresh and the land emanated a narcotic warmth, stronger than the *chillum* that Noor smoked at the camp in Dadaab. The corollas of the flowers reached Billai's bare knees, and I filled myself with the smell of the narcissus, transplanted to the island from the Green Ship months ago.

"Do you know why I like it here?" she asked as she lay down.

I shook my head.

"Because we're all immigrants from somewhere."

"If you think about it, Dadaab was also like that."

"But it's prettier here," she said, her smile showing disappointment.

I stared at her frail ankles. The first time I saw her at the refugee camp, she and two other girls were chatting while pumping water from a well. Each filled three jugs, two to carry by hand and one to balance atop their heads. They were three queens, models who strutted on dirt roads as if they were high fashion runways. She wore a long, colored skirt, a scarf on her head, earrings, coordinated makeup, hair in tiny, neat braids. Her balanced gait was perfect, her gaze ahead, noble, full of nonchalance. She shone with her own light, a star with black skin that emanated a supernatural aura as she passed, wiggling her hips between trash barrels, plastic waste, mismatched shoes, rusted pipes, and goats that grazed on what they could find.

We made the whole trip together. Sometimes, like in Sudan, I feared that she wouldn't be able to make it, like when we had to bribe the guy at the border. Or when she was hurt while we were crossing an area mine-laden by Boko Haram terrorists. But more than anything else, I feared for her life the night when two traffickers cornered her after realizing her beauty. She tried to defend herself, to stop the violence. She shouted for help, crying "Saidia! Saidia!" but nobody moved for fear of being thrown in the sea for defending her. In the end I couldn't stand it. I grabbed one of them by the neck and I flung him off the boat. The other kicked my back, grabbed my shirt and lifted me off the ground. I too would've ended up in the water had it not been for Professor Kysmayo, whose strong hands freed me from the grip of the trafficker and then threw him too into the dark waters.

"You're right, Billai...but unlike Dadaab, besides us all being immigrants, there's something else that makes me love this place."

"What?"

"That here, if we want, we can emigrate."

She took my hands and said in her solemn tone, "How it has always been and always will be."

Once in a while I talked with people back in Dadaab on the Internet. Nobody wanted to admit that the refugee camp–provisional since the 90s–had become a permanent establishment. Not the local functionaries who received funding to continue operation, not the United Nations that paid to not solve the problem, not the refugees, forced to live there without hope of leaving. I would never want to return there to survive, imagining a life elsewhere. My elsewhere, like that of many others, was being born from the commitment of all who participated in "No-Mad Land." If we'd created a precedent better than Sealand, the Republic of Minerva, Rose Island, to cite some cases Sergio had talked about, who knew what we'd be able to achieve? Who knew if international law would adapt to the fundamental necessities of humans?

My mother and brother were already on their way to intercept the path of the Green Ship. Professor Kysmayo climbed down to the islet and waved to greet us. In his other hand he held an envelope with a round object inside.

"Down there, did you see it?"

We stood up and followed him until we reached the top of another hill where there was a second meadow, green and flat.

"They taught me how to use the 3D printer."

White lines were traced into the side of the field.

"This is my first ball," he said, pulling the object out of the envelope and raising it above his head like a trophy. And then he gave the ball a kick.

A soccer goal awaited only us.

CELESTIAL FORMATTING

Translation by Georgia Emma Gili

An hour earlier

"So, it's set for today, then…"

Marina's body flows on a soft wave. The water streams over her and she absorbs it. Next to her, there's a man lying on his stomach.

"Yes, it's today."

"What a shame, I was enjoying this configuration."

The woman glances towards the rocks to her left. The mountain slopes sharply down to the sea. Some figures, like outlines cut against the opaque sunlight, throw themselves into the void, before re-emerging from the waves.

Marina takes off her t-shirt and floats free from a liquid which emits prismatic effects. With a twirl, she approaches Timo's angular face, as he lies on the sea shore.

"Time is not a variable which can be considered in our situation.

The drinks kiosk, a metal cube with lots of stringy spokes that cans, bottles and snacks are hanging from, looks like a sleepy spider. All around, crowds of seagulls stomp in search of food. Further up, immense albatrosses swoop in the sky like talking clouds.

Marina starts digging an ambiguous palm-deep trough around Timo with her hands.

I know, but I like *fluxing* with you. In three *animations*, we haven't done it that often.

Tactile sensation is something she can't get used to. Just like grains of sand slipping through her hands.

Far away music can be heard, from beyond the dunes and the Mediterranean maquis shrubs, imbibing their ears with exotic rhythms.

After the rain comes sun,
after the sun comes rain again[2]

Memories, whether fresh or indelible seem to be worth less to her with the passing of time. Sometimes, she even fears that they may dry up like the leaves of a perpetual autumn. Timo wraps his legs around his girlfriend.

"Do you want to regain lost time?

She lets him take hold of her hair, and that could be a reply to the question in itself.

"Tell me the truth; did you ever think it could last?

"Every time."

Surprised and full of disbelief, Marina looks at him askew.

Timo pulls himself up on his elbows. His girlfriend's hair covers his chest down to his belly.

"And all that interference? The connection was never that stable between us."

In his steady gaze shine the sparks of a sea chopped with waves of a perfect length and cadence, so harmonic as to be almost hypnotic.

Timo continues to observe the clear, compact, slate-like horizon. He's waiting for something to happen any second.

"Interference is part of our *relationship*. The thread can bend, but it won't break."

"Sometimes I envy your trust. You manage to spread it over everything."

Their fingers twist over their shiny bodies. And when they brush over their skin, they emit brief sparks and voltaic arcs of pleasure.

---

2 From the song *Underwater love* by Smoke City.

The same thing is happening all over the beach, even if the thousands of conjunction discharges are not due to the conductivity of the water.

"That's why you chose me from all those who were plaguing you with contact requests and *flux* proposals..."

Although he's usually harsh and tough, in this case he gives her a smile.

Like a puzzle fitting together, Marina's mouth matches Timo's.

You know how to take me by the brain. Right from the first day, at the Fiuggi site, at that wonderful spa."

"We were lucky... The same destination, compatible preferences and similar profiles. The difficult part came afterwards."

Their palms unite in a pair of hands. If it weren't for Marina's ivory coloured nail varnish, they could belong to the same person.

But then you make me angry, when you reduce everything to pure statistical facts! We are not only the result of an event which went well. We made our choices."

"Sorry... But you know I could be right. The way we met wasn't exactly romantic. I came from the Istanbul site, and you... you were so impatient to start experimenting. You risked connecting with a stranger. We wanted the same thing, at the same time and we needed someone to help us forget someone else."

From her wind-tousled hair, Marina extracts a scentless magnolia. The pink-streaked flower fluctuates on the watery liquid before reaching Timo's open fingers.

Still, you have made some romantic gestures, even in here.

"I hate missing the details of my animations."

In Timo's hand, the petals of the flower change colour, becoming ultramarine and just before turning towards

Marina, they become adorned with arabesques and inlays, special effects that Timo learnt to model during his stay at *Circeo Paradise*.

"I'll never forget you. Thanks to you, I've managed to live without going mad.

A dense mist comes up from over the horizon.

Timo breathes in without his nostrils sniffing anything different than the rarefaction of the air.

"I got here before you. You would have managed, even without my help."

The parameters around them are reconfiguring as they speak.

The curves which mark out the boundaries between their bodies and the other sunbathers break into numerous segments. All the colours fade into a lead-coloured blotched carpet.

"Is it starting? Is this how it always starts?"

The sun, instead of illuminating the scene, reverses a dark mantle over the area. The session dissolves into a *mélange* of shapes.

That's when Timo yells out.

"Save yourself. I'll do the same!

Thirty minutes earlier

A damp mist loaded with electrons slowly lifts towards a crimson sky. On Circeo Paradise beach a few pairs of bodies remain, stretched out and wet with a chrome-filled liquid.

The gulls have disappeared from the beach. On the other hand, the albatrosses dissipating above the clouds let out faraway screams.

Timo, I'm afraid. I thought I could make it, but it's all so absurd. Can we move?"

Both of them scrutinise the jagged waves in the distance.

"Being nervous the first time is normal and no, we can't move, it wouldn't make sense. It'll happen, anyway..."

How can you stand it, not knowing *when* it'll happen?"

Timo's pupils dilate to take in as much of Marina as possible. He wants to brand her on his memory at maximum resolution. It would be useful later, as they advised him to do, in a public forum on their condition.

"I just force myself to remember. It's the best way of holding on to you, and to me..."

She reaches out a hand and pulls a drink off the mechanical arm of the kiosk which Timo catches in mid-air. This gesture makes the beetle hanging from his collar sparkle which triggers a resentful reaction in Marina.

"You're mistaken, in Egypt, you almost forgot about me. Memories that are too perfect make us lose our sense of direction. I waited a week for you to get back in touch with me... And I couldn't have withstood it, if you had found refuge in *another site*, as you call it."

With his other hand, Timo caresses Marina's hips. This contact doesn't generate heat, and yet, it deceives perfectly.

It's been a long time since they possessed physical sensations. And they've even stopped asking where their memories really come from. They use a surrogate, a highly-sophisticated interface, to ease the structural limits set by the animation they've transferred into.

The billowy motion drives the water level until it laps against the lovers' chests. From behind the dunes of Circeo Paradise the melancholic notes of Portishead sound.

> *Wandering stars, for whom it is reserved*
> *The blackness of darkness forever*[3]

---

3 From the song *Wandering Stars* by Portishead

On the foreshore, every now and then scattered sparks light up, only visible from a distance. Then, a vaporous mist descends on all of them, just before that configuration is saved and is dissolved into nothing.

Five minutes earlier
"You have to force yourself. Concentrate and you'll be alright."

Marina's wide-open eyes are fixed on the line which separates her stomach from her hips.

"I can't. Just think of afterwards. Look, a piece of me...has already disappeared!"

A wavy shape is moving around under the skin of the water like a hacked-off eel's tail.

The deformation of Marina's body, like Timo's, is not due to refraction. There's something, in Circeo Paradise, operating at a lower level than perception. Something which is remixing their essences that they can't oppose.

"Everything will be okay. In truth, *formatting* is only a temporary transfer of data. We'll find each other again."

"Marina's breathing becomes shallower. She can't see her legs and only her head's left to imagine what's down there.

"How? Who will we be afterwards? And where will we turn up?"

"That's why you have to remember. That's the only way we'll be able to recognise each other in the midst of the channels. Please, Marina, your memory will unite us. Save the configuration..."

I'm trying! But where do all the memories go if the formatting wipes away everything?"

I don't know, but some traces remain. It's as if an echo of us manages to survive. Maybe, it reverberates in a buffer soul, maybe it's reflected into a plug area where the transmigration process loses data."

Everything at Circeo Paradise is now still and even the sparks have stopped crackling: the water level does not allow for further distractions.

I'm having trouble believing that you can exist after so many washes."

Marina's hands lift up and an ever-thicker liquid comes out of them. A lumpy substance which sticks to her fingers and drips off slowly. The outline of her hands seems blurred.

"I'm telling you it's like that. We have a contract and *we must* be maintained in a space of existence…All the spaces of this artificial hope are for giving us a possibility… the possibility of being rediscovered one day, by one another."

"That's nice, Timo, but it's very abstract and I'm afraid… afraid that something will go wrong and puff… goodbye forever."

"Listen to me, you have to remember every nuance, everything and every effect, only then can we live at a deeper level. That's why you have to engrave each other in our memories. I'll do the same."

"Live at a deeper level? What are you talking about? Can't you see? We're disappearing! We're dying once again…"

The air is filled with a tune Marina knows well. It's the start of *Scary World Theory*, the song that Timo always loves listening to after they've *fluxed*. Only now, instead of reassuring her, it sounds harrowing.

I've never said you'll have to
be afraid
of the cookie monster
beside your bed
It's not the real

> *The real one's in your head*
> *Beyond control*
> *The true one cuts you dead*[4]

Marina starts to cry and as she does so, she squeezes her eyelids shut so that her memory of that moment will be stored in the greatest detail, so that it can last beyond the present, wherever it is deposited.

One minute earlier

Marina's tense and lengthened neck makes her spit words into the air.

"I don't want to close my eyes and discover that you're no longer here."

The water, that has become a turbid mass, washes against their ears. When it slides into their ear canals, it feels as though their ear drums are frying: it's only one of the canals that they're about to be expelled from.

Timo tries to turn round, but the liquid laps against his nostrils.

"When you will open your eyes again... my presence will be so diffuse that you won't be able to ignore me or pretend that it hasn't happened.

"Timo, I'm scared! I've been afraid for so long that it seems normal. I can't stand it anymore... At this point, it's become how I react, how I think, how I breathe. My face is itching and I need to scratch, but I haven't got any hands!"

"Don't think about it... Fear often interrupts love, but sometimes love interrupts fear."

Grey droplets fall from the monotone cloak of the sky, corpuscles as light as ash. The first spots are forming on their faces, followed by deeper holes.

---

4 From the song *Scary World Theory* by Lali Puna

"Timo, I love you, but I'm still afraid.

"Save everything, Marina. Keeping saving, it's the only salvation."

Thirty seconds earlier

Circeo Paradise doesn't exist anymore. The level of chrome-filled liquid has become so high that the beach and all the dunes have been submerged. The condensed mist is the same colour as the water. The landscape reflects a wave motion cleared of human figures.

Can you remember everything?

A thought spurs Marina's sinking mind.

"Yes, but how have you managed?

The answer reverberates backwards in Timo's head.

"It's magic. You don't need your mouth, when you know how to manipulate certain frequencies. Let yourself slip underwater. Don't resist, you're only wasting energy. Go back to the peak where we spent our first New Year's Eve. Where we saw fireworks light up the rock in Matera.

Yes, we were the only ones there. That memory belongs to us, just as we belong to it."

"Well done...You've got it. We are like a river of memories that unwind in space and time. The forces that create its bends, depth and capacity are not only due to the territorial characteristics but also to the river's wishes. It might seem absurd, but trust me; I've been here twice before. At the next animation, you won't need to look for me; you'll need to look for the traces of memories of where we've been together, the events where our fluxes overlapped.

Their altered consistency has almost completely dissolved.

"What if I can't remember the right memory? What if I find someone else, someone with memories similar to ours?

"Stop whining and do as I say. *Green grass of Tunnel*[5]... Think of the song, sing it, sing it, sing it inside your head.

The wafting fog on the beach merges with the sea. In the space of a few seconds, the entire landscape dissolves.

A second earlier
Evacuation of the soul

Finding each other will not be easy and looking for a unique love-profile would take years, if not decades, before being concluded.

Timo and Marina, reduced to long strings of data, are two fluxes of consciousness unknown to everyone, except themselves.

Everything counts. Timo and Marina can't understand why, at least not yet, not till their next animation.

Individual memories would not solve the problem and finding *only* themselves would lengthen the wait. The solution is hidden in the power of shared memories, in the homeostasis of dispersed yet interrelated entities. In whatever conjunction would remain of them.

One second afterwards

"How did it go?"

Doctor Carigli approaches the lad pressing the keys of the holographic consol. With his callused hands, he is recalibrating the thousands of IP address values on the identity database.

"These logs can no longer be used. We need to reduce the bandwidth and the disk space on the server. We are receiving too many loading requests from Intensive Therapy and the Morgue."

He places his hand on the lad's shoulder.

---

5 From the song *Green Grass of Tunnel* by Mum

"Where have the new funds got to? They've been promising them to us for months. We can't keep them on hold for too long. They need to be *redistributed*.

Some piles of disks lay beside the lad. Each column a metre high. His gaze is bleak.

"I know, but they're stuck. They still haven't decided how to manage the growth in transmigration requests."

Leftovers of numerous lunches and dinners are scattered all over the office.

I understand, if you do notice any anomalies, let me know."

"I will, they'll be tighter, but they won't even notice

As soon as Carigli has gone, the lad puts on a song and starts singing *Street Spirit*[6].

Cracked eggs, dead birds
Scream as they fight for life
I can feel death, can see its beady eyes
All these things into position
All these things we'll one day swallow whole
And fade out again, and fade out again

Immerse your soul in love
Immerse your soul in love

---

6 From the song *Street Spirit* by Radiohead

Awakenings

translation by Sally McCorry

*We are increasingly dependent on prosthetics
and treatments to keep us alive,
but reduce our abilities to enjoy life.*
Serge Latouche

I am alive. The first image that floats up from my memory is the fuzzy shape of Marco's long gaunt face. My substance hasn't transformed into a story to be told. Something in my life must still need to be written.

Marco's reddish beard, with its streaks of ginger, has rusted in many places. Being reborn after such a long time has its advantages. I would like to reach out a hand and stroke this variegated hair I hold so dear, but I can lift no more than a finger. He notices and lifts his gaze from his phone.

"She's awake! Come quick. Eugenia has woken up!"

It must be Easter because in addition to the flowers on the bedside table, Marco is holding a chocolate egg. He puts it down, takes a damp cloth and wipes my forehead.

"Hello my love, what year is it?"

Hearing my voice is like dredging up a memory; like one of those things that have been neglected for so long you think they might not work any more.

"Hello Eugenia, it is 2048."

A machine has been keeping me alive for all this time.

"2048?"

The number shakes my identity, shocked by the knowledge that I am emerging from a deep abyss. I don't have the courage to add anything else. Marco's face is full of joy and relief; it would be unfair and selfish of me to wipe away those emotions, so I say, "How long has passed?"

"Nine years."

Another number I cannot get away from: thousands and thousands of days, an infinite number of grains of sand have slipped by without me having lived them. The only consolation is that the flow was slowed.

I look towards the foot of the bed but I cannot see my daughter.

"Where is she? Sara must now be ..."

I can feel the floor vibrating with the footsteps of someone running. The shaking comes from my ankles, rises up my calves and just brushes my thighs.

"Eighteen years old!"

A shrill voice yells from the entrance to the room.

I barely recognise her. Between the Sara I remember and this adolescent there are many children and young ladies. A whole deck of identities time can not give back to me. She is wearing a black s t-shirt, its short sleeves fringed, as if ripped. Her hair is long, hanging loose to her shoulders, (she used to hate her hair like this and would ask me to tie it up in a ponytail) and a pair of showy earrings, dangling metal spirals like whirlwinds, which light up intermittently. I get the impression they are recording the scene in realtime.

"C'mon, what are you waiting for? Come and give me a kiss."

She starts towards me instinctively, but then hesitates, and in the end doesn't move. She turns to the side and I notice someone behind her.

"May I, mum?" Sara asks a stranger.

An elegant looking woman, about forty, nods, the hint of a smile flashing across her face. I remember when I used to wear my hair like her, when I was younger: an impertinent fringe highlighting cheekbones and jaw.

I welcome my daughter in my arms, I hold her tight and sniff her neck.

"Mum?" I whisper in her ear. "What's that all about?"

Husband, daughter, mum... After nine years it is as though the concepts shaping our relationships have faded into simple words and have lost their strength, crumbling and becoming vague, generic terms that are no good to anyone. If you don't watch out, they can be lost for ever, whether you like it or not.

"Don't worry," Marco says, and starts opening the Easter egg. My heart races. When he has finished unwrapping it he holds it out, offering it to me.

"Why do you say that? Should I be worried?"

I take the egg but don't know what to do with it, so it rests in my hands as if I am trying to hatch it.

"We... well, at the time, when the accident happened the doctors didn't know... when or if you would wake up..."

There is guilt in his voice. The implicit admission of something to be ashamed of. Nine years are long enough to put anyone to the test. I drive all these thoughts out of my head. I don't want to ruin my reawakening so soon.

"Well, now you know. Who is she?"

That woman isn't a stranger. My daughter just called her mum.

What does Marco call her?

On the other hand my life has only just started running again, whereas theirs never stopped. When I used to read a book or watch a film, I would feel like I was following the thread of a precise plot, giving substance to my idea of the story, but what happened when I wasn't reading or watching? What did the characters do without my eyes to watch them?

Marco looks first at Sara and then the stranger behind her. That woman has a familiar face, well looked after, a trace of makeup, not a hair out of place; now I was paying her more attention, I wouldn't say she was much more than thirty.

Over time any space tends to get filled. It is only to be expected. I just want to understand how it happened ...

"Sara was so sad after the accident. She didn't want to go to school any more, she spent hours and hours in the bathroom, she didn't even want to go out with her friends, she had practically stopped eating."

I grab my daughter's hand. She is wearing nail varnish. The same colour as the mystery woman's.

"I'm so sorry. I remember rushing out of the office, the network wasn't working. A general blackout... The people walking along the streets were panicking, then a car ... driverless. Drove right into me without slowing down. I remember the crossing's stripes on the ground, almost completely faded."

The spread of pain: it extends vertically, along the family axis and horizontally along the temporal one. Technology doesn't soften the intensity, it spreads it out.

"Are you OK now, my love?" Luckily she nods.

Marco sits on the bed next to me and rests a hand on my thigh.

"Who is she, are you going to tell me?" I am not easily shocked and I don't like public scenes. Above all, I don't understand what reaction I should have, faced with this apparition: anger, dismay, jealousy? The woman hasn't said a word, she has done no more than smile.

"I bought a mourning management service. She is you, with an artificial body."

"What? A service... Me?"

I pull my hand away, a reaction of uncontrollable disgust.

"Yes, she has your personality, rebuilt from a cerebral scan. She is an Artifical Intelligence who has relived all of your experiences right up to the day of the accident ... since then she has been emulating you."

I shudder at the idea that for nine years a machine has been looking after me and another has been taking care of my daughter. Should we be grateful or pity our physical and psychological fragility?

"She... emulates me?"

"Don't be angry, Eugenia. It was supposed to be a temporary form of therapy, psychological support for Sara to help her get over the trauma ... but then nine years passed."

I cover my mouth to stop the scream coming out. I struggle with the absurdity of the situation. Is it how Marco says, or is this artificial intelligence, this anthropomorphic icon modelled on me, supposed to compensate for my physical absence and comfort him too.

"If it was temporary, like you say, she can be turned off?"

"Yes, of course we can do that."

Sara turns to the other woman. My daughter is shocked and scared, a breath of anxiety escapes her lips. Every time my gaze rests on her I see two people: the child of the past, and the nearly woman she is now. I cannot resolve them into one image.

The *other Eugenia* frowns, analysing the data.

"Think about it though," Marco hurries to say, seeing things are taking a turn for the worse, "Sara has spent more time with her than with you."

"So what? What do are you saying? Wasn't she just an emulation?"

"Yes, but... you would be killing her mother again."

Mother. That word, naturally associated with me from the moment of her conception and for all of her gestation, from her birth through her nursing and growing up, has slipped away a day at a time. It has slipped away from Sara's thoughts too, a little piece at a time... and that emptiness has been filled by another Eugenia.

"So that makes her the mother? He presence negates mine?"

"No, of course not."

"Then maybe you would just prefer to send me back into a coma? Or leave me here?"

"What are you talking about. Nobody wants anything like that."

The egg I am holding is beginning to melt form the heat of my hands. The chocolate has got all over my fingers. I lick them to clean them. "Gianduia. It's delicious."

I offer the egg to Sara, she has always loved chocolate. She breaks off a big piece, the other Eugenia does the same thing, and Marco takes what is left.

"She can eat?" I ask without looking directly at it.

"She doesn't assimilate, but she can simulate," Marco answers jokily.

Licking her fingers Sara asks, "Couldn't we all just live together?"

I take the box with the Easter egg surprise in it, and put it on the table.

No one wants to open it.

Wylmar Jail

The moon is full tonight. That doesn't make me the monster they say I am.

I can hear Friso, trotting along behind me on his short legs. They caught us together, while we were downing a couple of tankards of beer, but he's not guilty of anything.

The stars stay outside when I cross the prison threshold, at the peak of Mount Wylmar. Two guards walk me down a corridor. Every time I try to slow down they prod me with their halberds with such enthusiasm that anyone would think I'd defiled their daughters.

They shove me into a cell. Friso they leave outside.

To tell the truth, I didn't rape anyone.

The jailer is waiting in the corner, in the shadows. He doesn't greet me, just looks me up and down with his rheumy rat eyes. He's condemned me already.

"C'mon, strip and take that shit off."

That shit is my life. I know they'll give me the harshest sentence. I know those High Court sons of bitches will take everything I have earned in my life, except maybe my identity. Although, as things stand, it only takes a glance at the worldwide ratings to realise that, right about now, my identity's worth less than nothing. I'm the lowest of the low, after having tasted the dizzy heights of the top of the ratings for a month.

Friso the dwarf glances at me disconsolately, his watery eyes and taurine neck straining in my direction. He's not allowed to come any closer. The shadow of his big nose brushes the bars of the cell.

"Like I said in Court, I was tricked. Something must have gone wrong with the analyses…"

It's no use. Off comes the silver helmet, adorned with erotic scenes to distract enemies. I won that from the Basilisk of Constantinople in a game of cards. Down goes the double-bladed axe, spoils of my victory at the Joust in the Bowels of Pestrem. Off with the chain mail shirt, stolen from the Master Smith Berengario and, without a doubt, the thing that has saved my life more often than my wit alone could have done.

The jailor couldn't give a fuck about my complaints. He collects my things, stuffs them into a nondescript crate and makes to go. Before he does, though, he can't resist the chance to further humiliate me.

"I'm only carrying out the sentence of the High Court of Criminal Justice for Role Playing Games and Crimes against Avatars, so you have no right to look at me like that. My hands are cleaner than yours."

I shouldn't be angry with him. Today it's my turn. Today I am the Bogey Man. This *incarnation* I've worn for so many years won't be around much longer. Having come so far, I'd thought – hoped – I wouldn't have to ever abandon it. It'll take a lot of luck before I can show myself around again, because I'll be starting up from the lowest level. I may as well play the part to the full.

"You might be following orders, I'll give you that, but I see you put some enthusiasm into it, all the same."

He pauses at the entrance to the cell.

"It's my job, if you hadn't noticed."

"That's the difference between us. I'm playing the game. You're working, so show me some respect."

"Respect, you say? Look where your respect for the *game* has got you."

He doesn't give me the chance to reply, just slams the door and leaves.

The crash – the hollow boom of iron on stone – reminds me of many good times, memories of a life well-lived. Those thoughts that are interrupted when Friso asks the guard for the crate.

"I'll pay you well for it. I mean, he's not going to need it for who knows how long."

Sadly, my dwarf friend gets no answer. I would have preferred my worldly possessions to have gone to him, my old drinking companion, rather than see them sold off in some village fair from the back of a tinker's cart.

I lie down on the damp floor, scrape together some straw for a pillow, and suddenly the memories are back. Shirez, for instance. He abused his dominant position and, in a moment of folly, proclaimed himself sovereign of the Under Cloud, in contempt of the local Dungeon Master's rules. Then there was the elf, Yaroslav – poor mild Yaroslav. Once a hunter of werewolves and lost treasure, he had ended up accepting the lowliest of missions. He had exterminated rats, saved cats stuck in trees, even mucked out stalls – anything to remain somewhere among the ranks of the living players. And how could I forget Laryon, the half-blood orc who killed himself with the same blade that had forged his shining career, unable to bear the shame of being captured by the cowardly Kai'Pun while taking a shit in the latrines of Ilisander.

Who else could I add to the list? There was Yelena, of course, that dark-haired beauty. She had never made a secret of the fact that she used her charms to her best advantage. She would boast shamelessly of turning a profit from any magical spell or enchanted trinket that found its way into her sweet hands.

Just before drifting off to sleep, I swear I would rather die than lose my Assassin's dignity.

The acrid stench of stale piss keeps company with my last thoughts as I drop off. Truth be told, my crime, that slanderous accusation they claim has discredited my name and will bring me to ruin is, in my mind, a source of pride. I am Sandor the Assassin. The name I bear cannot be taken from me, not by stripping, divestiture or declassing. As for that treacherous seductress known as Tessa Zerven, well... she's going to die.

The High Court of Criminal Justice for Role Playing Games

The next time the cell door opens, it's morning. The jailer wakes me up with the tip of his boot.

"C'mon Assassin. Your moment of vainglory has arrived."

In his hand is a mass of chains. He hurries to fasten them around my ankles, wrists, and neck. Heavy rings link them together and, when I take a step, I make the same sound as a cook rattling her pots and pans.

The sun is rising as we step outside the prison. I walk along acting humble and docile. The winter daylight is lazy and slow in coming, but still it dazzles my eyes, forcing me to keep them lowered.

We pass through a wide door that creaks on ancient hinges. The darkness once we're inside the place lifts my spirits. I'm not one to complain, but what I cannot stand is the charge of sexual assault stuck up on the noticeboard at the top of the stairs leading to the Court. It's true, I struck Tessa, but she wanted it. I mean, she's always liked doing it like that. All they'd have to do would be to check a couple of things, and even an idiot would be able to see that the sex and the violence didn't happen at the same time.

The jailer leads me like a dog on a leash. He takes me to the second floor, Courtroom 201, then sits me down on a bench.

"Don't move. If you aren't scared enough, look up there."

Four gargoyles preside over the court. Their all-seeing eyes flicker in the shadows, veiled by the curls of smoke that twine around the scrollwork on the ceiling.

At first glance, Courtroom 201 appears empty. However, as soon as my eyes adjust to the gloom, I can make out the silhouettes of a fairly large number of people filling the curved tiers of seats. I know at least half of those present either by reputation or because of my line of business. Elf thieves, trickster magicians, treacherous Amazons and usurious dwarves, all have come to enjoy the spectacle of my end. In one way or another, we are all part of the game. You don't just come and go from the worldwide rankings. Reaching the top is tough and, once you get there, you'll do anything to stay.

After one minute, the Dungeon Master makes his entrance. He's the henchman of who knows what occult power, hooded administrator of justice dressed in malachite and black. All those present rise submissively. A bunch of hypocrites waiting to take my place. An exhibition of public derision, shamelessly thrown in my face.

Sure, we all want to earn points by working less and killing more. Every one of us wants to make it to the next level without having to sweat too much. Still, selling out like this, wholeheartedly embracing a sentence that stinks of duplicity without conceding me so much as a shred of defence... all I can say is, that's not my idea of justice.

They've made themselves into defenders of a false morality, every one of them. They take the side of the judges and hand down sentences to people like me – people who are just trying to earn a good reputation by skinning dragon tongues and cutting off werewolf paws, smashing zombie heads and ripping out vampire hearts. Meanwhile, they sit in their rooms, all happy and content, refreshed from getting fanned by their servant-concubines. They make and break other people's ratings, handing out bonuses and penalties between aphrodisiac cocktails and plates of roast goat.

The way I see it – and it's not because I'm sitting here in chains in front of a bunch of cowards, swindlers, and traitors – is that people who can do something, do it. People who can't just criticise and talk shit.

"Does he know his sentence?"

The Dungeon Master isn't talking to me. He's whispering with the jailer.

"Not yet."

I can read lips. It's an Assassin's talent – a level-three skill.

I know the Master. He's an old hand, famous for swallowing law books and coughing up sentences. He's the same guy who was handing me my missions a month ago. He used to like to set me impossible tasks and make me complete them in a day. He's also the guy who decided the amount of gold and number of seals I earned when I got to the end of each level. So, you see, it doesn't come as a surprise when he lifts his gavel and hammers it on the lectern.

He gets his silence.

From above his bald head, the withered arm of the Profiler descends at his command. A screen lights up on the wall and, on it, the whole of my life begins to unfold.

The Dungeon Master accesses the Avatar Levels and Attributes Reconfiguration System, striking fear into the hearts of all those present.

Cue the anxious muttering. Cue the smirks of satisfaction.

The double helix of my DNA frames the data of my present incarnation.

It must be thirty years since I last died.

"What you must know is that this is Justice in action."

At this point, the spectators would love to hear the condemned man moan, but I refuse to give them even this small pleasure.

"Sandor Kernoy, do you understand the shame of what you have done?"

I will not beg for mercy. I don't want anyone's pity.

A deeply brooding expression mutely crosses my tormentor's face and settles there, as though carved in stone. Meanwhile, upon the Profiler, cut in sharply edged characters, my sentence appears: 0.

With a wave of his hand, the Dungeon Master gives permission to proceed. Two guards grab me, lift me bodily and drag me to the centre of the Court. There, the Profile Block stands ready to receive the rings of my binding chains.

"By the powers vested in me by the People of the Game, I pronounce you fallen. I hereby strip you of all titles, talents, seals and any and all lands and property you have obtained during the course of your present incarnation."

The jailers force me to kneel and lower my head, pushing it down until my forehead is touching the rough, oily surface of the Block.

"Justice without honour is worth nothing! Find out the facts before you sentence and condemn someone!"

The surface of the Block is concave. That's how many people have bent their heads on it.

"Receive your just level. Accept it as your punishment. This is what your actions deserve."

It is then that the revelation becomes manifest. It starts with my eyes and spreads from there throughout my body. My fingers, a network of scabs and callouses, shrink, becoming soft and smooth. Patches of abraded skin, shiny as gemstones, vanish. The scars whose stories have often entertained my companions around the fire all disappear. The forearms, so rough and muscular, become hairless and plump.

I regret the loss of everything about my old body.

My powerful thighs become slender, my chest narrows, my shoulders seem to wilt. I am no longer the hard man I was. I have gone back to being a child.

An Assassin with milk teeth.

I struggle out of my ridiculously large tunic, its size no longer my own.

The courtroom is silent. I pity every inch of this callow new body.

Zerven Palace

I've spent whole nights perched on top of town-hall gargoyles, unceasingly alert whether exposed to the pouring rain, the lashings of the North wind or the beating heat of a midday summer sun. I explored every nook and cranny of the sewers of Anshan fortress until sickness settled in my chest. I have fired arrows at flying hippogriffs until my hands cramped.

From among the branches of the Blue Sequoia I have climbed, I look down into the space behind the defensive wall. One of the many Zerven brats is busy fucking around in the garden, whistling a funny tune, singing a rude little ditty.

I fit a stone in my sling.

My nerves had been reduced to a handful of boiled noodles, but now I'm ready. I once tracked the Yeti across the Khorder glaciers until my feet were frozen. My old knees were wrecked from chasing leagues and leagues after the rumour of a unicorn. It is therefore with extreme pleasure that I now jump from one branch of the Sequoia to the next, confident in my newfound agility as I seek out the best spot from which to strike.

With these sharp young eyes, my prey has no chance, even if he's not my real target. My true quarry is Tessa Zerven, that treacherous weaver of falsehoods. Thanks to her marriage to the magician Daryush Cardissian, she has become the princess of the contemptible Kai'pun – a fitting role for one such as she.

Nonetheless, I have to act according to plan.

I hit the little bastard square in the forehead and he falls to the ground on the spot. Five seconds later, fat screaming maidservants are running to his aid. The wound isn't lethal. It's just a bloody little warning that one of them will refer back to their slut of a mistress.

Next time, I'll pay her a personal call. She won't recognise me, but even so, she's still my wife.

The Inn at the Sign of the Wild Boor

The Wild Boor has always been a place for a good time, where I could spend a few carefree hours. I find Friso next to the brazier, downing yet another pint of cider. I always know where and how to find him. He's sitting there, wrapped up in a fur-trimmed cloak, with a couple of ugly mugs I've never seen, both as short and stocky as he is.

They're playing dice, and my hanging around is making them twitchy.

"What the fuck are you looking at, kid? Haven't you ever seen how dwarves eat breakfast before?"

He rubs his hand over his dripping beard, then stuffs a lump of black bread into his gap-toothed mouth.

I point at his cider. "Let me have a swallow."

He bursts out with a hearty laugh, then lifts the tankard like he's gonna throw it at me. I don't move.

"Idiot of a gnome! It's me."

He looks me up and down. I'm wearing a shirt I stole from a peasant's laundry line. On my feet are a pair of clogs I claimed from a street urchin after a fight.

"Me who?"

"Sandor. I'm serving my sentence in this body."

"Maybe I've been drinking, but I'm sure as hell not crazy. Don't fuck with me, kid. I'm not in the mood. Now fuck off before I crush you."

Instead, I move closer to him and put both elbows on the table. The other two dwarves must not like it much, because they look daggers at me.

"You've got to help me, Friso. I've been expelled from the Assassins' Guild."

"What are you talking about, kid?"

I grab him by his filthy cloak and shake him with adolescent brutality. He looks almost rattled. Then I flick his sleeve into the air, the empty one.

"Your arm. You lost it going up against a pack of Grey Wolves."

"What a surprise! Even the walls know that."

He drains the rest of his cider.

"C'mon then, you big-nosed fool... Ask me something!"

He's dumbstruck. No one calls him that but me. Friso doesn't let anyone make jokes about his longest appendage. Still, with the way things stand around here these days, he can't afford to believe his ears.

"Alright, you little fleabag. Tell me, who's the best whore down at Sparks Tavern? It'll be ten years before they even think about letting you in there."

I don't need to think twice.

"Leona Longtongue. She's always been our favourite."

His eyes pop, then he throws himself at me, squeezing me with all the might a single arm can muster.

"I'll be damned. Sandor! The ways of the Dungeon Master are truly infinite."

I free myself of his grip and hop up onto the edge of the bench. The other two don't say a word, although one scoots over so he can keep on eating in peace.

"Bravo. Now order me a pint and listen up. You remember that witch of a wife of mine?"

"Is that even a question?"

"She has to suffer, then die."

"Have you looked in a mirror lately? You? Against an enchantress? She got the better of you when you were a grown man. What do you think she'll do when you're no more than... what? Eleven?"

The Baths of Beryon

I'm on a roof. Pulled by a medium-sized elephant, the litter moves in fits and starts through the thronging, bartering crowd. The amber curtains flutter, revealing an ankle decked in sparkling bands. Perfumes of sandalwood and lemon waft up to caress my nostrils. The object of my revenge is lying there, waiting to go to the Baths of Beryon, as she does every Tuesday morning.

Friso is waiting too, in position at the rear of the building.

The litter stops in front of the entrance, the curtains part, and Tessa steps through them onto the foot board. She is not so much beautiful as she is disturbing. She's the kind of woman you want to slam against the wall and take, just like that, just for the pleasure of wiping that superior smirk off her face. Her olive skin and Oriental eyes tell of ancestors from the steppes, but mixed with more temperate Nordic blood. It's cold outside, so she's wearing a heavy woollen dress, adorned with studs.

A squadron of handmaidens form a cordon to help her make her entrance. As soon as the procession of women and eunuchs disappears inside, Friso goes into action, with me right behind him. While the dwarf amuses himself flirting with the servants at the entrance, I crouch down and slip in behind him. I manage to sneak beyond the counter and keep on until I come to the corridor that leads to the women's section.

I pull a turban out of my bag and wind it round my head, then I put on a short, flower-patterned cotton tunic, cut for a girl. My youth and unfinished features work together to make me androgynous. Dressed up like this, it wouldn't be hard to mistake me for some matron's spoiled daughter or a lady's sickly niece come to take the waters.

I take a moment to sneak a peak at the curves of the half-naked women, wrapped in scraps of silk that cling to their skin. Their sweaty transparencies augur well for the success of my plan.

I peer into the different pools, each separated from the others by inlaid wooden planking.

"Sorry to bother you..."

"I've lost my lady..."

"I don't suppose you've seen Lady Zerven, have you?"

So relaxed are they that none are bothered by my intrusion.

I wander through saunas equipped with incense diffusers and a solarium that doubles as a massage suite in the winter. I finally find her in a Turkish bath. Large bellows keep the coals glowing. The scents of juniper, resin, pine and frankincense fill the air.

Tessa is facing away from me. One girl pours water over her head from a golden jug, while another rubs her back with aromatic ointment. A third weaves flowers into a leather thong to make garlands.

If I hadn't already been sure it was Tessa, I would have recognized her by the tattoo on her neck, the symbol of The Order of Necromancers. It was one of her hag friends who advised Tessa to take up with them. It didn't take much effort to talk her into switching her class once she had abandoned the Assassins' Guild.

I should have known that I woman I'd found in a brothel would never lose the habit of doing whatever it took to achieve her ambitions. Indeed, such a woman will shift course to attain them more easily. It was I who was hired by her father to save her from the horrors of her imprisonment and rescue her from her captor. That abductor was none other than that same Daryush Cardissian who passes himself off as a magician, when all he is in truth is an common slaver with a black magic fetish – and now, her lover. It was I who became the latest victim of her boundless desires and never-ending lies.

If I place forgiveness and revenge on each side of the scales, which one weighs more?

I married her and brought her to live in the ancient home of the Guardian of Wylmar. I opened the doors of the Assassins' Guild to her. I helped her rise to the 50th level, introduced her to the best Role Players in the Cloud Community and – as if all that that weren't enough – I took her everywhere with me. By my side, she walked the snowy trails of the far Indranùm mountains, the desert roads of Silandia... and what did I get in return? Betrayal is a coin that Tessa spends often and willingly. I have no doubts that what she did to me she will gladly do to all those who come after.

I go back out and look for the trunk where her clothes await. I rummage through the bags until I find the key bearing the coat of arms of the house of Zerven – the Ouroboros of the Order of the Healers that Tessa could never stand, because it reminded her of her father. I pull out the tub of wax I prepared in advance and press the key into it. The impression will go to my friend Xazù, armourer by trade and burglar by nature.

I put everything back in its place, then stick my head back in the door, careful not to let the steam out. Speaking in a shy falsetto, I lay my trap.

"Shall I change your aromatic oils?"

One of the handmaidens turns. The steam is so thick that my face, transfigured by the Profiler's sentence as it is, is impossible to see clearly in any case.

"Change it, but wait... What do you have?"

The girl comes over to me.

"We have three fragrances: refreshing Fermano citrus, juniper oil and camphor, or a laudanum blend, with mandrake added as a stimulant."

She repeats the whole sentence for her mistress, who doesn't even bother to turn around.

"The last one, the blend..."

Never trust a label. I make the phial of laudanum and mandrake vanish with a conjuring trick. Into the bowl go the contents of a different phial – aniseed and nutmeg – that I'd been hiding up my sleeve. When the maidservants turn round to check, I flash a sly smile. Then I close the door and seal it with my own padlock.

I count to five. I feel a bit sorry for the maidservants' stomachs, but much less so for Tessa's, which will soon be twisting and cramping from the aniseed. The fun part of my little payback is about to start.

It's a pity I can't stay and see Tessa's face when she's overcome with nutmeg-induced hallucinations. Still, I'm not going to deprive myself of the pleasure of hearing her scream, at least once, before making my escape and removing my disguise.

"Arrghh! Catch that girl!"

That girl is no more.

Wylmar Residence

An Assassin is never where he would wish to be. He's always with his victim, even when he's not in his hunting grounds. When he's at home or tending to other affairs, his thoughts are never far from his prey. In my case, there is an added complication. I was thrown out of my home by the woman who is both my enemy and my next victim, Tessa.

I've found a place to bed down behind Friso's shed. He likes to see himself as a dwarfish knight errant and, as such, doesn't care for the commodity of a fixed abode. When I go in to wake him, he's still snoring so loud it's making the boards of the old shack creak. I've never met anyone else capable of making such a godawful racket.

"It's nearly sunrise. Time to kill."

I hand him a burlap sack. There is a smaller one inside.

"Give me a chance to wake up, will you?"

"Boo!"

He jumps and shakes himself all over.

"You've got to be worse than some pesky damn kid."

"C'mon, let's move. Delivery's in an hour."

The bed stops groaning the moment Friso transfers his weight to the floor.

He pulls on a pair of horsehair trousers. He pulls his belt tight and breaks some encrusted sludge off his boots. I hold the door open for him. He throws his cloak around his shoulders with a disapproving huff.

Outside we gather up some branches from Lanoor Oakwood and make our way to my – now Tessa's – house.

When we arrive, we find a line of tinkers on their carts, alongside bloody-handed poachers, drunken mercenaries, and travelling troupes of mummers ready to offer up their services in the form of tragedy or comedy. There are jugglers, minstrels, alchemists, and ugly mugs of all sorts, races and colours.

The maidservants from the baths are alive and well. In fact, they're darting in and out among the throng in search of good deals. When the haggling gets long and tiresome, a pair of eunuchs with painted eyes and varnished nails give them a helping hand, finding fault with the merchandise at hand, complaining about this and that, chipping away at the price and negotiating quantities.

Tessa's shopping list knows no bounds or limits.

I can see ampoules of bitter tamarisk, rare white hellebore seeds, and a violet-tinged liquid that looks like dillwater, glazed plums, pineapples packed in barrels of ice, short-haired lemurs, skins of wine from Lush and antique Kolkon amphorae. Not even my first wife, Kendra, was this bad. She left me because I was never at home, not because I was an Assassin. Women don't care what you do for a living, as long as it's no skin off their nose.

Once I've climbed into the smaller sack, Friso settles me in amongst the pieces of wood in the larger one and flings the whole lot, me included, over his shoulder. Wood for the fireplaces of the Wylmar Residence passes through the gates with ease. Tessa hasn't got the time to attend to the basic needs of the place, and neither do her maidservants, given the quantity of tasks and range of errands they have to cope with.

Nonetheless, at the gates there are two guards with plumes sticking out of their helmets and crosswise pikes on their breastplates.

"What's in there?"

Friso stops and sets me on the ground, feigning weariness.

"Firewood."

"Wood, you say? Let's have a look, then. A guy came two days ago."

The armiger unties the knot and opens the sack. He rummages around with one hand, just brushing my knee, but the sack is so deep that he can't reach down to the bottom.

"I live near Lanoor Oakwood. I collect firewood every day."

I hear more footsteps. The second guard is suspicious. I can see a shadow and then the point of a spear comes down and starts piercing the sack.

"I keep some back every week to sell."

I put a hand over my mouth, squeeze my eyes shut and clench my teeth in pain.

"You sure these aren't the usual damp twigs?"

Friso bends and pulls out a log, showing it proudly to the guards.

"You call that a twig? This wood burns hotter than a virgin's ass!"

They all laugh.

"But at least wood don't scream!"

More laughter. So, this is the level of security in my house. It's enough to make me happy – almost happy – that I don't live here anymore.

It's night when, with a Kliss blade lent to me by Friso, I cut through the burlap of the sack. I'm aching all over after eight hours scrunched up in a corner of the cellar.

The first thing I do, with immense relief, is to piss on the wood. Even if I can't have my powers back, access the list of missions put out by the Assassins' Guild or bid on an assassination job posted by the Dungeon Master, I'm still not quite ready to hang up my dagger. Whether said dagger belonged to me or someone else mattered almost nothing before, in terms of effect on the rankings, and it matters little to me now, on this quest for noble revenge.

I've always loved hiding, ever since I was a kid. Every time someone came to our house, I would run and look for some nook or cranny to hide in, or a bed to slide under and become invisible. With time I honed my hiding skills and, over the course of the years, I learned many ways of creating diversions. I used to be fast, too, training myself by catching rabbits in my aunt's yard. Perhaps this new body, young and unused, will give me back my lost agility.

"Light as a shadow, silent as a feather", or was it, "Silent as a shadow, light as a feather"? I don't know, I read it somewhere. In any case, I go up the stairs to the second floor. I'm hit by a wave of nostalgia as I go past my own personal Trophy Case. In the darkness of the corridor I recognise the outline of the skulls of Manilon, the last of the three-headed Dragons of Ostralia. I swallow my bitterness and move on.

I'm about to slide Xazù's counterfeit key into the keyhole when I notice Tessa's door isn't locked. Once inside the cavernous room, where the darkness is absolute, I sense something malevolent – something I slept next to for six years.

Tessa hates the light and it only takes a sliver of it to wake her. Every time my bladder would force me out of bed, I'd find it difficult to get my bearings. I used to bash my knees and stub my toes, but noises didn't bother her. Tessa would have gone on sleeping if I'd set to sharpening my knife. It was only light that bothered her.

I move towards her, but furtive noises drift in from the corridor. Slippers slide along the floor and a voice whispers. I expect it's the servants, meeting late to give each other some measure of release.

I slip along the wall. A tiny flame insinuates its light through the crack around the door and she, as if she can feel it tickling her face, shifts in her bed. No one here wants to wake her, though for different reasons. The light vanishes.

I count to twenty and then unsheathe the dagger. I can feel my heart beating, a pounding that knows no reason. The sentence of those charlatans of the Court is an outrage that can only be washed away with blood.

Tessa is lying sideways beneath the canopy of her four-poster bed. Her expression when sleeping is peaceful, the exact opposite of the face she puts on when she is awake and always wants the last word.

On the day of the alleged rape, driven by the endless verbal sparring, I lost my temper and I slapped her. Then I slapped her again, and again until the pain of it finally shut her spell-spitting mouth. What had happened before that, however, had been our own way of exorcising relationship problems. We would hurt each other – brief moments of reciprocal pain that would make things better in the long run.

I pull back the sheet, ready to strike, and hear a sharp hiss, of the kind only a forked tongue can make. My wife is sleeping with a snake in her bed. Her guardian's sudden movement wakes its mistress. Tessa's eyes open wide, showing bewilderment at the sight of a child facing her, a dagger in his hand. With a quick swipe I decapitate the viper – the small one.

"Surprise!"

"Who the hell are you?"

She mutters a few abstruse words and her hands take on a red hue. Two balls of fire form on her palms.

"Your husband, sort of."

"Sandor?"

She is caught off guard and she fires without waiting for an answer. She knew I would come back in the body of a child, but she thought I would also have a child's mind. For my part, I'm dumbfounded, because I didn't think she could go so far as to sleep with a snake.

Caught in a storm of fireballs, I'm forced to retreat. My hair is on fire and I can feel my skin already charring beneath my smouldering clothes. I throw myself towards the curtains. I hope I have enough time to open the window before Tessa can recharge her smoking fingers.

The second round grazes me as I sail out and down into the moat full of filthy water. It puts out the flames, along with my foolish ambitions.

Friso pulls me out with a big fisherman's net. He drops me on the grass and helps me strip off my sodden rags.

"That wife of yours is just like a sword. You've got to beat her again and again while she's hot to make sure she's forged right."

Dwarf wisdom.

The Forest of Phoenixes

There is little else I want other than to render Tessa powerless. Call it revenge if you like. For me, it's payback for what she's put me through.

Now she knows that what she's dealing with isn't just the threat of a frustrated kid. Neither is it a game for points or levels. The day after my discourtesy visit, Tessa wasted no time before fleeing the Wylmar Residence like a thief in the night. She tried to get there, but she never did manage to reach the Polyandro Isthmus, the finger of land where Daryush Cardissian has built his castle. Well, at least she didn't get there in quite the way she planned to.

Four of us followed her, riding two ponies. Friso and I were on one, Fleabag and Babyface – his stocky friends – on the other.

I knew Tessa would run to her magician. What I didn't know was that our ponies would be able to keep up with her stallions.

Friso strokes his animal's mane.

"These beasts don't know the meaning of fatigue. We raised them in the darkness of Dumuria as draught animals. They're the only living creatures capable of going into the mines and coming out again alive. They hate sunlight, and at night they run twice as fast."

Nonetheless, when we end the chase in the middle of a clearing in the Forest of Phoenixes, on the evening of the third day, the ponies are exhausted. For hundreds of years, this forest has been a stark place – acres and acres of dying trees and nowhere to hide. Under a ruined tower, where Tessa and her garrison camp to refresh and water their horses, we've laid our trap.

Friso has brought his double-bladed axe out from under the bed for this ambush. Managing to get your revenge is like a birthday, a rare occasion to be honoured. He sniffs with that notoriously big nose and keeps an eye on Tessa's half-stunned guards. His dwarfish partners are keeping watch on either side of the clearing to ensure our escape.

They had been gathering firewood to heat their yurt: Tessa's magic is powerful, but it doesn't last the whole night.

When we've finished hogtying them, necks to ankles, I can't help but speak to her.

"You filthy witch. This world is full of cowardly, hypocritical men and sly, conceited women, but you all love to dress yourselves up as heroes and heroines."

"They'll catch you and make you pay for this, too."

"I know. There's no place for me in the worldwide rankings anymore."

"Do you really think you are any different from me and the others?"

"You threw me to the Court."

"They will catch you again."

I don't want to listen to her words so I wrap a piece of cloth over her mouth and tie it tight at the back of her head.

"It doesn't matter. I know what they'll do to me this time."

I rest a gentle hand on Tessa's horse. She mutters into her mount's flank, but no magic words make it out of her mouth. The reins pull and tighten around her neck.

I have never felt so alive.

Tessa brought me back to this ever-spinning circus, to this farcical carousel of ups and downs, but if I hadn't played the game, what life would it have been?

With or without the nightmare of the Profiler, would it have been worth it?

I slap the horse's rump. It rears, neighs, and sets off at a gallop as if I'd put spurs to it. Tessa goes off at a gallop too, her mount dragging her along behind.

The sound of its hooves masks the snap of her neck and proclaims the dynamics of the accident to the world. She'll make it to the castle of Daryush Cardissian, in the end.

Court of Criminal Justice for Role Playing Games

When they knock on the door of the shack, I don't run. I open it and hold out my wrists for the Court goons, who take me back to where this story started.

"Gentlemen of the Court, the Profiler does not lie. I have committed many crimes, some greater than others, so many that I remained at the top of the worldwide rankings for a month. Someone paid for these misdeeds. The traps and the tricks, the extortion and the thievery were all committed in the course of fulfilling contracts legally recognised by this Court. Never did I sack an inn, lay waste to a home or raze an entire palace when I wasn't on a mission for a client. I don't deny it nor do I repent. I have killed and tortured. I have exploited and abused the defenceless simply to gain all the points I could and rise through the levels. Nonetheless, it is equally futile to deny that an Assassin lives inside each and every one of us."

Murmurs of disapproval provide the background noise for my words.

"Sandor Kernoy, spare us this rhetoric of a cornered beast. You speak of deeds commissioned by the Guild and contracts for the Dungeon Master. These useless digressions not only waste our time, they insult our intelligence. This is not the reason why you are here."

"Then what am I accused of this time?"

I pretend I don't know. It's part of my defensive strategy, just like when I pretended to be shocked when they took me from Friso's shack without even giving me the time to put my clothes on – always assuming there is a way to seem less guilty when facing the Dungeon Master.

Some clown in the shadows of the Court's loggia ventures a sarcastic quip. I can just make out the quiet sniggering, the almost-amused whispers. If it were up to me, most of these scum – the disdainful elves, bewitching fairies, and two-bit magicians – would be guarding pigsties, breakings stones in a mine or spending their time cleaning latrines.

"You stand accused of violating the sentence decreed by the Profiler."

"That sentence was unjust."

The judge looks at me impassively.

"You are also accused of having taken justice into your own hands, without the backing of either Guild or Dungeon Master."

"The *first* sentence was unjust."

"Even if the first sentence was unjust, the second certainly shall not be. You have had your vengeance."

There is yet another trap hidden amongst in the Dungeon Master's words. I can feel it tightening around my current incarnation, an existence marked by an adolescence as brief as it was undesired. So, they allowed me to act, but why? To what end?

The Profiler makes its horrible appearance once more above the Dungeon Master's head. What can possibly be worse than level zero? What can there be that goes beyond the erasure of every effort and the deletion of everything achieved in a lifetime?

I look at the double helix of DNA framing the Profiler and get an inkling of what might be my next and definitive sentence.

"Bring the goblet."

It feels as if they have pierced me with a whole quiver of arrows. I remain standing, but when Daryush Cardissian emerges from the shadows holding a golden goblet, I am perturbed.

He proffers it to me with a bow bordering on the ridiculous, half-way between adulation and mockery. There is the hint of a smile on his face as I stare at the goblet. I don't know what I'm supposed to do with it. It doesn't seem right to hold it up and I don't believe I have won anything.

He doesn't stop smiling until, with a flick of his eyes, he indicates I should look inside it. Now I understand.

Daryush Cardissian, the Court's magician, has brewed the potion roiling in the goblet with his own traitorous hands. It is full of a genetic poison. Then I understand the rest of it. I see that this never was the story of my revenge, but of his.

Against Tessa? Against me?

With a single stroke, Daryush has freed himself of us both. Though I can hardly blame him for the former, I have my objections to the latter. Nevertheless, it is obvious that, where there are rankings, there is competition and, where there is competition, the rules vanish.

I bring the goblet to my lips and taste its contents. The liquid is milky and cloying. I take a swallow.

He stands beside me and, from above, encourages me to swallow the rest with a light pressure of his hand.

After just a few moments, the Profiler's genetic frame begins to crumble in places. I feel a bit dizzy. My lips become numb and I lose sensation in my throat.

If addiction is the dark side of pleasure, then deactivation of the SCN9A gene is the radical cure against the very definition of humanity. The genetic sequence flashes around the frame of my existence – until it goes out. No emotion, no pain. On the outside I may be vegetable, but inside I will be no more than mineral.

From the Courts to the brothels, from the inns to the barracks, every so often my story will be told. People will inevitably tell of my end. They will say that, all things considered, it was a foreseeable conclusion. Still, when it comes down to it, what would life be if without games – some clean, some dirty – to pass the time?

Two Worlds

translation by Sally McCorry

> *Humans are here today because our particular line never fractured – never at any of the billion points that could have erased us from history.*
> Stephen Jay Gould, Eight Little Piggies: Reflections in Natural History

From the repaired chronicles of Kilimanjaro

Aruna turned to say good-bye to her parents, opened her arms and lifted them to free the plumage. She stretched out her neck, breathed in deeply, and let her calves lift her. Her torso was exceptionally ample, well suited to supporting her for a long time.

She was about to take-off for the Flight from the shelter of the Solar Tree, three metres outside the Shining Corolla. In a line behind her were the faces of many friends, tense, nervous, and distressingly thin.

The song of the Aeromancers, arranged in a semicircle for the Ceremony of the Flight, could be so hypnotic as to make you believe anything. The horizon that called her to maturity flattened into an opaque strip, infested with clouds of ammonia. Below her a 15,000 metre drop plunged down to the static mass of the Global Ocean.

Old Canderum of the Purple Feathers finished explaining the goal of the Flight for the thousandth time, then solemn and haggard approached Aruna. He bowed his enormous beak to one side in a gesture of good luck, and stopped singing. With a gentle push to the back of her neck, he cast Aruna into the emptiness.

"Fly, Aruna! Fly towards hope!"

Canderum's shout announced Aruna's eighteenth birthday, when for the first time she would leave without having a precise destination.

The young woman dropped, together with another fifteen companions from the Solar Tree Major and perhaps none of them would ever return. Like everyone else who, year after year, had participated in the Ceremony.

Aruna closed her eyes, folded back her wings to gain speed, altered her trajectory and let the ascending currents take her westward.

Going back empty handed would be a terrible dishonour.

Mnemonic relic 1 (source uncertain)

Not even the supercomputers had been able to predict that the hybrid genes would react so quickly and fill so many ecological niches. A number of sequences were dramatically defeated in a competition rendered ruthless by human alteration and an evolutionary process that had been going on for millions of years.

Other sequences, a tough minority, took advantage of this situation to adapt, and incidentally, evolve into forms of life that from then onwards, populated the Modified Earth.

The "human race" in the form it presented before the Second Ecopoiesis, no longer existed. In their place, there were two races whose DNA shared 99.96% of their genes with the human race, but no longer walked the Earth.

Because they had not discovered intergalactic flight in time to populate new worlds, human beings had discovered a way to bend the barrier of time and conserve their lives for centuries. When the human genome was decoded in the Second Millennium, scientists were surprised to find that it consisted of a mere thirty-five thousand genes. They had expected there to be more. Not least, because even a worm had twenty thousand.

So they enriched that sequence – a string of three billion letters formed from an alphabet of four elements containing the instructions for building and maintaining a human body – with a number of additional codes that would provide some highly desirable qualities: qualities useful for adaptation and survival, values that were commonly found in species other than the human one. Chimeric experimentation was the beginning of the end, it was when everything was mixed up together. The cancellation of the 2005 "Human Chimera Prohibition Act" was approved in accordance with the idea that the principle of human dignity should be applied exclusively to the individual and not generally to the whole species.

Even before chimerism, it was common practice to exchange human cells with animal cells: cows secreted human proteins in their milk, human blood ran through the veins of pigs, and sheep were the recipients of human liver and heart transplants. Vice-versa, many human beings possessed cardiac valves derived from pig and bovine hearts.

Still, the phenomenon that followed chromosomic liberation – known as Genetic Confusion – was also the basis of our salvation.

It was in fact demonstrated that there were no true genetic barriers between the many different species, and the proof of this was in the fact that the human genome code clearly showed the presence of a genetic continuity between all the *animate beings*.

The thick high containment walls that had for millennia kept species separate crumbled within a few decades. The very idea that genes were insurmountable barriers to human adaptability was shown to be unfounded.

The Aeromancers learned to fly and oxygenate their blood better, enabling them to settle on the arid mountain tops. The Aquamancers became glabrous, acquired from fish the techniques of obtaining oxygen from water, and populated the seas.

This reconstruction is the result of a research study into how to ensure the survival of animate beings.

From the repaired chronicles of Saxayé

On the twelfth day of nonstop flying over the Global Ocean, after having travelled 11,000 km without having come across land, nor even a log to rest on, Aruna let herself fall, skimming over the surface of the sea. Exhausted, she succumbed to weariness.

Her worn out body, dehydrated and close to death, was intercepted a few hours later by a reconnaissance patrol who had never seen an Aeromancer before, except in the films taken from underwater they had been shown when they were still at school.

Drawn to the surface by a floating shadow, Karia, Co-orny and Tsai Chin, moved cautiously closer to the creature with feathered arms and a beak instead of a mouth: the shape was of an *animate* like they were, even though there were evident differences, like the rows of nails on her hands and feet, more like talons than their own webbed fingers and toes.

The bright wings folded behind her arms like drapes were a rainbow of green, yellow and red stripes, but now dirtied with dust and dulled by marine contamination. Keeping away from the slicks of oil, Karia sniffed the stranger, and turned to Tsai Chin, the patrol's leader.

"Do you think we should take her down below?"

"I don't know, it could be risky."

The youth's narwhal like face looked worried. Although he was quick to act, Tsai Chin thought carefully about every decision.

"But we have to help her ... She's dying."

The girl's beak was withered and blackened. In some points, it shone like mercury.

Little Coorny looked towards the horizon and grimaced. Not only was there a storm coming that would generate fire twisters, but his nose could detect the stink of an enemy approaching, closer and closer.

"Quick ... That *orcark* knows exactly what to do with her."

Hearing their conversation, the girl regained consciousness and opened her beak.

"I'm looking for the Tower... Do you know where the island is? Please... I have to find it, help me."

Then she was quiet, overcome by her exhaustion.

A big bubble of hydrogen from below reached the group and took them a few metres higher. Karia grabbed hold of the girl.

"What do you think she was talking about?"

"She's raving, maybe she's ill."

Tsai Chin's prudence had made him head of the team even though he was so young.

"I reckon we should take her down with us. Iguain will know what to do."

Karia, on the other hand, was naturally curious. Her webbed fingers were expert in investigating coralline encrustations and fields of kelp; she loved swimming with the fish and wandering amidst the iridescent seaweed. Whenever she could, she would set off to look for giant crabs and velvety sponges. She loved the spores, microbes, and even the viruses.

Life under water was prolific, and she had fun riding rays, flying on the back of mantas, and drawing with the cuttlefish and octopuses.

"We don't know her, Karia ..."

Tsai Chin blinked his nictitating membranes uncertainly. Then the air valve in his neck vented vigorously; Karia smiled.

"All right then... But you're going to guard her. Your father will decide her fate."

Coorny took a breathing kit out of his pouch. Even though they had never taken an Aeromancer back before, they knew what they had to do.

After uncurling the tube, Coorny placed the mouthpiece on the girl's beak and the oxygenating bands behind her shoulders. The bands' tiny fissures, acting as artificial gills, would allow the outsider to breathe underwater.

The orcark continued to approach with its characteristically comic movements: its head rocking drunkenly. It was probably its hunger that made it look so ridiculous.

The patrol formed a diamond: Tsai Chin in front, Karia and Coorny on each side, and the outsider last, towed by her arms. They dived quickly, heading towards Saxayé: their underwater bubble.

They stretched out their fins, and accelerated together.

With bloodshot eyes the orcark, its mouth hanging open expecting to feed, missed its prey and resigned itself to going hungry yet again.

Mnemonic relic 2

Though all the entrances to Saxayé were dug in the sand, the tunnels stretched and branched out across the seabed for several kilometres. Air was pumped into the large corridors and the domes through porous walls made of osmotic membranes that absorbed oxygen from the sea water, releasing bubbles of carbon dioxide in the process.

Saxayé was situated close to two hydrothermal vents surrounded by prolific colonies of 5 – metre long tube worms, 50 cm bivalves, and an abundance of prawns and mussels.

It was a complete ecosystem based not on photosynthesis, but chemosynthesis. The hydrothermal vents were the ocean's alternative to the old power stations. The springs also served to purify the salt water. As the water penetrated the Earth's crust, it lost minerals, was cleaned, and released back into circulation by the thousands of steaming vents.

It was an incredibly slow process, but the Aquamancers were in no hurry, they preferred efficiency to imbalance.

The supporting structure of Saxayé, anchored to the seabed by stainless steel chains, had made the inflatable city the most economic structure for providing space for the growing population of Aquamancers.

References were found in the distributed memories of the supercomputers to a few populations on the east coast, who mindful of time spent underground during the war, had started to install these structures as temporary dormitories for immigrant labour.

What for the Aquamancers turned out simple to get up and running again, having access to technology they had found surviving in watertight depots and laboratories, turned out to be disastrous for the Aeromancers.

They had had to find shelter in the few Solar Trees left standing, surviving on inaccessible semi-desert terrain which had resisted the rising levels of the Global Ocean. Forced to live on land that was arid and as hard as rock, their population had remained stable for centuries. This meant though that any chance or unforeseen event could easily compromise their survival.

Growing food crops was only possible at a certain altitude in plantations reaching out towards the sky to make the most of the weak solar heat: cassava, sweet corn, peppers, beans, squash, and potatoes could be harvested up to an altitude of 3,600 metres. Between 3,600 and 5,000 metres, only potatoes would grow. Beyond that, every plant, even though modified by ancient biotechnology, stopped yielding any fruit.

According to local myths, the Ice Age had lasted for about 500 years, an exceptional phenomenon that had occurred at least another two times. Yet according to the same legends, when the climate stabilised again, the tundra would recede and the parting waters would uncover fertile lands, and the Aeromancers would be able to come down from their heights; the heaths would flower again and their Solar Trees would prosper once more.

They had been waiting for this moment for centuries.

From the repaired chronicles of Saxayé
Karia entered the med-lab pushing the gurney at speed.

"Dad, we found this girl. She was floating in the Ocean, almost dead."

The stout shape of Iguain Celcantoss turned first towards his daughter, and then towards Aruna. She had regained consciousness, but however hard she tried she still couldn't make her talons clasp.

"An Aeromancer? And the rest of the flight? And what was she doing in the sea?"

Iguain picked up an oblong device from the work top and ran it over the girl's body. He stopped at her shoulders, where the inflammation was visible.

"There wasn't anybody else. She mentioned a Tower ... and an island. She said she had to find them."

The Doctor's smooth face was rapt with concentration as he checked the readings. He turned to the Aeromancer. For centuries the inhabitants of Modified Earth had been using the oceanic language which had become the repository of idioms and dialects from before the Second Ecopoiesis.

"Can you hear me? What's your name?"

She nodded, and tried to grab his arm. At the sight of her talons Iguain dodged out of the way and the young woman's hand dropped. The bone structure of her arms was very elongated, especially near the hands where the metacarpals and phalanges were twice as long as those of an Aquamancer.

"My name is Aruna Dalkey, of the tribe of the Aeromancers of Kilimanjaro."

Iguains's cutaneous crests suggested he was smiling. Though after a while Aruna realised that that was almost a fixed expression on his face. The feathers along her arms quivered.

"You are not going to die... you're just very tired. How did you manage to get this far? We're 11 days travel from the nearest coast."

"8 days... if you're flying."

He opened his eye membranes wide, exposing aquamarine irises. He was honestly surprised, as if Aruna had said something nonsensical. His surprise though owed as much to seeing an Aeromancer after such a long time; the floating bodies they sighted always ended up as food for the orcarks if the fire twisters didn't reduce them to shreds first.

"I'll give you a solution to drink that will make you feel better."

Iguain proffered her a container and Aruna drank the oily liquid. It was only then that she realised she was in a med-lab.

"Where am I? And who are you?"

"Welcome to Saxayé, the capital of the Aquamancers. My name is Iguain Celcantoss and this is my daughter Karia."

"Saxayé? I've never heard of it... But thank you for all you have done. Now I must continue with my journey."

As soon as she tried to get up, the doctor stopped her.

"It's too soon to fly. You need to rest..."

The doctor's manner was thoughtful and considerate, and Aruna didn't want to seem rude or discourteous.

"Let me go... Before it's too late. I have to find the Tower."

"In your condition you wouldn't even be able to beat your arms for even a minute. I don't want to keep you here against your will, but trust me, it's better if you build up your strength before taking off again."

As soon as he turned away to put his instruments on the work top, Aruna could control herself no longer and burst into tears.

"You don't understand... My people are dying. Only the Tower can save us."

"Wait, calm down. Tell me about this Tower. Why are you looking for it? And why is it so important?"

Iguain Celcantoss handed Aruna a handkerchief. The Aquamancers, as far as airborne reconnaissance had shown, were peaceful people. Aruna needed to be able to trust someone. Anyway, Karia had saved her life and that had to be a good sign.

So the Aeromancer told them everything about the threat hanging over all of them, and hoped she wouldn't live to regret it.

Mnemonic relic 3 (source uncertain)

At the beginning of the third Millennium, near the North Pole, on Spitsbergen, an island in the Svalbard archipelago, a building was erected that was known to the future generations as the Tower of Seeds.

Inside the Tower, thousands of samples of all the different varieties of seeds were stored in the hope that one day they would in this way be able to survive an accident or natural catastrophe.

Following the Second Ecopoiesis, the island sank beneath the Global Ocean and from then on no-one heard any more about it. Despite this, the vault's construction and the care taken over its security led many Aeromancers to believe that if they could find the Tower, they would still be able to use the seeds.

According to various mnemonic fragments, the Tower, powered by a thermopile, consisted of three rooms located at the top of a 125 metre long tunnel. The seeds were kept at -20 degrees Celsius and sealed in specially designed containers made of four layers of aluminium. These containers were stored inside canisters and placed on the shelves in the vault.

The low temperature and humidity levels in the Tower would limit the metabolic activity of the seeds and keep them integral. Preserved correctly, some seeds could last for millennia.

From the repaired chronicles of Saxayé

Aruna and Iguain meeting had unhoped-for consequences, the most important of which was their audience with the Council of Saxayé and its outcome.

The president, Yecené Urus, in his official uniform, a fluorescent overall with an opening on the back for his dorsal fin, had listened in silence to the words of the outsider, but he wasn't convinced.

"If I have understood correctly, you are saying that the existence of the Global Ocean is under threat if we don't find this Tower?"

Aruna was standing in front of the members of the assembly. Her plumage had regained all the vigour of her genetic line, and shone with a myriad of colours. She found Iguain's presence by her side reassuring. The medic, for some reason, had believed her. In fact he seemed almost happy to be helping her.

His cutaneous crests were more tightly stretched than usual, frequently revealing his conical white teeth.

Together, Aruna and Iguain had spent hours and hours sifting through the available mnemonic relics hunting for information about the location of the Tower.

The Aquamancers' network was not extensive, and lots of scouts explored the submerged ruins to hook up to old databases.

The fact that she might be the only survivor of that year's mission kept a faint flame of optimism alight in Aruna. She and her companions had left the Nest without knowing what to do, nor how to proceed if they had succeeded in finding the Tower.

Their flight was more a test of faith than of hope.

"Yes, that's right. The disappearance of humanity caused, amongst other consequences, the evaporation of the coolant reservoirs of about 870 nuclear power stations scattered around the world and the meltdown of their reactors. The clouds that continued to form for decades afterwards turned out to be more of a problem than the radioactive material. 500 billion tons of methane deposits were released as the layers of ice they were trapped in melted. All that gas accelerated global warming to levels that had been unheard of since the end of the Permian period."

"This data is known to us. There are no boundaries between the ecosystems. The ocean is no longer constrained by the limits imposed by the continents and it no longer has the divisions it used to have. The Global Ocean was the origin of everything that breathes and reproduces, and it seems that it is also their future. We see no threats on the horizon."

The round head of president Urus nodded up and down. The members of the assembly approved.

"Permit me to disagree."

Aruna turned from one side of the semicircle to the other. If the Tower really existed, and the Aquamancers could be convinced of the danger they were all in, maybe they would be able to help her.

"Have you ever left the sea? Have you ever analysed the situation of the Risen Lands?"

Some members of the assembly gasped, others vented their air valves. Some, irritated, whispered to each other. Who did this outsider think she was to throw around accusations, how dare she seed amongst them doubt and fear about what the future might bring.

"The Risen Lands? Are you referring to the lands made hard by the Ice Age where you have made your nests?"

"Yes, before the Second Ecopoiesis, below the mountains, the lakes and the river deltas were suffocated by weeds and fertilisers. The green film on the surface of the stagnant waters transformed into tons of algae that could absorb so much oxygen from the water that anything swimming in it died instantly. Our ancestors witnessed everything from above. When the algae collapsed from the lack of oxygen, their decomposition intensified the process. The lagoons, once crystal clear, became great expanses of sulphureous sludge; the river estuaries spread for hundreds of kilometres in unending dead zones. The plants and animals survived according to their tolerance to UV rays, or mutated beneath a bombardment of electromagnetic radiation."

Aruna closed her eyes. Her beak beat the words out with force. The Aquamancers kept listening.

"When the worst happened, life went on. It went on regardless, even though the parameters had changed. We, the animate races, are the result. Now though, the threat still hangs over us because there are no more trees left to defend us."

"What have the trees got to do with the disappearance of the Ocean?"

"Like I said, our ancestors, on their first flights, saw everything from above. Their genetic memory preserved the memories of those events in the chemical composition of our plumage. If you don't believe my words, check the analyses against the fossils of the birds from the First Ecopoiesis.

Aruna turned to Iguain who lifted a translucent plate.

They had come prepared, knowing that the Council would insist that they look at the matter in a totally rational manner.

"All right, continue... We want to know about the trees."

"The disappearance of the trees together with heavy use of engineered seaweed to produce fuel hydrogen once the fossil fuels ran out, caused the Earth's temperature to increase, and in consequence the level of the Ocean to rise. There is a limit beyond which the biosphere ceases to provide protection from the effects of these types of processes, and starts to magnify them instead. The only way we can save the Earth is by replanting trees. The clouds will give us water once more, and the Sun will heat and produce vapour from the watery mass of the ocean. This is the only way the Global Ocean can be made to recede and the Risen Lands become fertile again. With the seeds from the Tower, we will have seasons again. Do you even know what seasons are?"

The Aquamancers remained unmoved, like when you listen to an explanation about the mysteries of the universe, and the sheer size of the phenomena exceeds our mental capacity to comprehend them. It was difficult to read their expressions

Aruna hoped she had managed to get the message across.

Mnemonic relic 4 – (source: Wikipedia fragment)

The Maunder Minimum is the name given to the period that lasted from 1645 to 1715 of the First Ecopoiesis, when sunspots became an extremely rare occurrence. The phenomenon was named after the astronomer E.W. Maunder, who discovered the absence of solar flares and sunspots during that period by studying the news of the era. During the Maunder Minimum, astronomers recorded 50 sunspots, instead of the more usual 40,000 or 50,000.

The beginning of the Maunder Minimum was abrupt, with no warning phenomena, though during the final phase, between 1700 and 1712, the sun's activity gradually picked up again and began to increase.

The Maunder Minimum coincided with the coldest part of the so-called little Ice Age, during which Europe and North America, and perhaps also the rest of the world (for which reliable data is not available) suffered particularly severe winters. Data from successive eras led scholars hypothesise that during the Maunder Minimum the Sun might have expanded and its rate of rotation diminished.

From the repaired chronicles of Saxayé

At dawn of the following day, a squad left Saxayé heading northeast towards the banks of Bioluminescent Plankton. Behind them the inflatable city looked like a 25 km long boomerang.

The inhabited corals exploited special organisms to agglomerate cemented sand structures connecting the underwater archipelago with mobile bridges floating at varying heights.

The fish that swam around it all could see Saxayé steaming and gurgling amidst thousands of bubbles of CO_2 in suspension.

Iguain had taken the place of young Coorny, while Tsai Chin had been moved down the squad's formation to Karia's side.

Aruna, unsuited to swimming, was transported in a capsule that was so narrow that to fit she had to fold her arms around her upper body. Their destination was a point near the North Pole. According to the mnemonic relics, this was a plausible position for the location of the Tower.

Iguain had managed to convince the Council to grant him permission to accompany the outsider, verify the entity of the threat, and "take possession" of the seeds. The risk that the legend might be true and that the consequences foreseen by the Aeromancers were a real possibility, must be taken seriously. Still, Iguain was not sure what meaning to attribute to the expression "take possession".

He had a plan too, but of a completely different kind.

In the past, he had heard rumours about the Tower, but that information, like many other things, had been forgotten, until Aruna's story had brought it back and reactivated it.

Near Miami, the squad came across thousands of eels like silver ribbons, up to five metres long swarming with graceful agility thanks to rudimentary fins and their pointed snouts.

When they dived into the deeps, they saw the trail of pilings that had once held up one of the human civilisation's motorways. Following these, they reached a merchant ship resting on the seabed and half buried in the sand, its corroded iron hulk feeding a prolific mass of multicoloured seaweed. All around the wrecked ship, amidst statues covered with anemones, spores, and starfish, spread a ten centimetre thick carpet of red seaweed.

They decided to set-up their bubble and stop to rest.

Mnemonic relic 5 – (source: Wikipedia fragment)
Whoever wants to access the seeds in the Tower must get passed four doors: the entrance, a second door in the tunnel, and a further two airtight doors.

The keys are coded in such a way as to allow access to various levels of the structure, but not all the keys open all the doors.

Movement sensors are present all around the site.

A work of art makes the vault visible from many kilometres away. The roof and entrance are covered with highly reflective mirrors and prisms designed by the artist Dyveke Sanne. This installation acts as a signal by reflecting the polar light in the summer months, whereas in the winter a network of 200 fibre optic cables illuminate the site with a colour changing light, varying from turquoise-green to white.

From the repaired chronicles of Saxayé
On the third day of their journey, while they were eating their evening meal, a mixture of crustaceans and mollusks in a sauce of coral mucus, Tsai Chin lifted his head from his bowl.

The coral formations they were camped in had cracked the road's surface and invaded the surrounding buildings. The streets had been engulfed by a covering of bright green moss.

"Can you hear that too?"

They all turned to face the rocks. At the top, the outline of the crumbling skyscrapers stood out, with manta rays as big as ancient aeroplanes flying between them.

Aruna's hearing caught no sound vibrations, but the Aquamancers ground their teeth. Then Aruna jumped, she too could now hear the low repeated laments. The sounds that at first had seemed mournful, after a little changed in their intensity, and became grunts, punctuated here and there with whistles and murmurs.

Sharpening her sight, Aruna could make out a pair of *Megawhales* passing by a few kilometres away. She guessed that the one in front was the female with the male following behind, performing complex sound modulations in his courtship of the female.

"They're going north. We'd better hurry up..."

Karia said, and Iguain started to gather up their things.

"How can you tell?"

Aruna turned to the young woman who was helping her father, while Tsai Chin was listening raptly to the hypnotic frequencies of the Megawhale's song.

"I recognise the song. It reaches 68 Hz. The songs of the Megawhales are different depending on where they come from. Look at them, they are the largest beings on earth."

"No, they're not ... You should see the Giant Sequoias, they can grow to be taller than a hundred metres and weigh up to 200 tonnes."

Iguain opened his eye membranes wide, and stared at Aruna.

"There are Giant Sequoias on the Risen Lands?"

"They were crossbred and made resistant to the climate. We have three on Kilimanjaro."

The Aquamancers settled Aruna into the capsule and stowed their air bubble. Tsai Chin took out some slender ropes and started using sign language.

"Let's hook the ropes on. They'll give us a lift and we'll shorten our journey by a day."

From the repaired chronicles of Saxayé

At dawn of the seventh day, beyond the Krill Fields, Aruna saw what must have been the beginnings of the fjords.

Later, half hidden by teeming underwater life, she saw an encouraging sight.

The images in the mnemonic relics that Iguain had shown her matched those from her childhood. Drawings, paintings, and graffiti that portrayed the Tower decorated the walls of the Aeromancer Academy and the Corolla of Solar Tree Major.

Her people's dilemma consisted of having to make the terrible choice between sending its children out in search of the Tower, or hoping that it was all a lie, in other words, the choice was between weakening the Nest or else seeing it destroyed within a few generations.

As old Canderum had explained to her, the decision to continue with the Ceremony of Flight was linked to the fact that legends needed to be valued according to their capacity to generate "morale" in those who stayed behind, rather than on the basis of their truth.

Because of the Flight, the life expectancy of the Aeromancers was much shorter than that of their ancestors, though they had overcome part of this disadvantage by becoming sexually mature at an earlier age.

They generally reproduced during puberty so the population had not shrunk as much as the elders had foreseen. The strongest individuals were excused from procreation, because of the risk they were to run. Candrum was known for saying "It is better to raise heroes than orphans."

However, it was also plausible that the Second Ecopoiesis was hurrying along their natural selection, increasing the probability that the new generations would be born with a greater tolerance of radiation.

The Aeromancers knew that they were a transgenic form of life, which had evolved to face an extreme and continually mutating environment. A mutation that was guarded inside the Tower now before Aruna.

The squad was moving forward holding its formation when Tsai Chin realised that below them an intertwined mass of plants was rising rapidly. It was an enormous macrocyst of kelp.

"It will block the entrance if we don't hurry."

Iguain motioned the group to move swiftly so that they were not crushed by the mass threatening to engulf them.

"Swim up!" was the next sign he made to Tsai Chin, who vented his air valve as hard as he could.

"No, we'll waste time."

Tsai Chin pushed the capsule with Aruna in to the head of the group to help the three Aquamancers push their way through the columns of seaweed.

"It's not common kelp, Tsai Chin. It's carnivorous and will rip us to shreds." Iguain's mouth was clamped shut.

"In these latitudes? That's absurd..." Tsai Chin shook his head, he couldn't believe that the seabed could rouse itself and grow before his very eyes.

As Iguain knew, courage didn't always make up for inexperience.

Less than twenty metres from the Tower, a compact wall of lianas forced them to slow down.

"It's been crossbred with something, and I don't want to know what with..."

The lack of oxygen in the area around them, so quickly sucked out by the kelp, would cause them to suffocate within a few minutes.

Iguain distributed the breathing kits to gain a little time, but as soon as he did, a spongy tangle enveloped Tsai Chin and dragged him down with it. Karia pushed Aruna ahead of her, while Iguain stopped and watched Tsai Chin armed with a dagger fighting those roots. If he went to help Tsai Chin, he would put the lives of the others at even greater risk.

Tsai Chin took out a bar of sodium, which on contact with the water burned incandescently amidst a cloud of bubbles. The kelp, alarmed by his resistance, called up even more tentacles.

At the sight of this, Iguain kicked his legs, beat his dorsal fins and resisted the tenacity with which the kelp was trying desperately to survive. When he could no longer see Tsai Chin, Iguain filled his lungs, pushed with his pectorals, and swam away, helping his daughter and Aruna to safety in the narrow entrance of the Tower.

Mnemonic relic 7 (source: paper fragment)

The most alarming thing is that we have no idea about the mechanisms which enable a natural phenomenon to disrupt the Earth's temperature with such speed. As Elizabeth Kolbert observed in a mnemonic relic from the New Yorker, "No known external force, or even any that has been hypothesised, seems capable of yanking the temperature back and forth as violently, and as often, as these cores have shown to be the case. [It seems] like some kind of vast and terrible feedback loop." We are a long way from understanding all of this.

From the repaired chronicles of Saxayé

The metallic walls of the Tower had not been colonised. Partially stained by sponges and lichens, they reflected a small portion of light, even now from twenty metres below the surface of the Ocean.

Shaken by the loss of Tsai Chin, Iguain pounded his fists on the Tower's door to the disbelief of Karia and Aruna. It was madness to think someone would come and open the door, nonetheless a display lit up by its side.

"Welcome to Spitsbergen island, I am the Custodian of the Vault, its security AI, how can I be of service?"

The girls came closer, intrigued. The supercomputer was still working, though it was not up-to-date with the situation on Modified Earth. The island no longer existed, covered by the Ocean.

"We have brought some seeds we would like to deposit."

Aruna shook her feathers, a gesture typical of her race. She opened her beak angrily and pounded her hands against the capsule.

"You've got seeds?! And you didn't tell me?"

As soon as the doors opened, the three were pushed in by the pressure of the water. When they stood up again, after the doors had closed, they found themselves in a corridor sloping 20 degrees upwards. Emergency lighting indicated which way to go.

"I'm sorry, the Council forbade me from talking about it. And anyway, it was the best way of getting us in."

"You lied to me..."

"No, I do have some seeds, but they are as old as fossils."

Iguain opened a bag and showed Aruna the contents. A strong smell of rotting hit her. A slightly sweeter version of the stench that was also already present in the corridor.

The internal surfaces of the Tower were covered by a film of dust, and as the AI led them closer to the top of the vault, the smell became the stink of mould.

When they reached the Seed Room, they could not hold back their disgust and horror: their hopes lay there rotting in an unending series of carefully labelled containers.

"They're all rotten! The seeds are useless... We got here too late."

Karia put her arm around the visibly upset Aeromancer. To return to the Nest only to tell her people that the seeds had turned to dust would throw everyone into deep despair.

"That is not exact. Some have survived."

The AI opened a door at the end of the Room, and inside a few of the cases, some names lit up: Himalayan Cedar, Caucasian Elm, and Whitebeam, and then Rhododendrons, Azaleas, and Magnolias.

"The Barley seeds decomposed after 2,000 years, the Wheat seeds after 1,700, but the Whitebeam will last for another 10,000. You can leave your seeds here, I will take care to preserve them until the time is right for a new planting."

Aruna ran to see close, drying her tears as she did so. Iguain, laid down his package and was about to move away when she grabbed him by the arm.

"Where are you going? We have to get the seeds. We haven't come all this way to leave empty handed."

Iguain's eyelids dropped from the tops of his eyes until they were completely covered. The absence of eyelashes made him look strange to the Aeromancer.

"The aim of the mission was to verify the existence of the Tower and identify its position. Someone else will decide what to do with the seeds. We will report back to the Council and tell them what we have discovered."

"But my people need these seeds. We must take them back with us!"

"The Council will use its judgement to decide what to do with them. If it were not for them, we would not even be here."

"I know... but the seeds don't belong to anyone. The seeds belong to the Earth, and they must be returned to the Earth. The seeds are like the force of gravity and sunlight, they existed before the human race came along, and continued after its disappearance. No-one can <u>own</u> them."

"This is a decision the Council must make."

Aruna let her beak hang open, then tilted it to one side and unfolded her wings threateningly.

"No Iguain, this decision belongs to *you* too! We are alone here, and I don't think that you came all this way, at your age, only to satisfy your curiosity and to put a cross on a nautical map."

The Aquamancer vented his air valve. It was difficult to carry on doing his duty, now that he *knew*. The existence of the Seeds was a truth that could put his dream of repopulating the Risen Lands into motion.

When he was a boy, Iguain had loved to swim to the surface and gaze at the sky. The star fish were nothing compared to the stars that floated high above. During the night, under the spinning constellations, hypnotised by their mysterious movement, he would ask himself what was up there.

On the edge of the outside world, he had never plucked up the courage to take the last step, the step that would have taken him out of the Ocean.

In the years that followed, his mind was often filled with thoughts of the Risen Lands. It was as if his memories held, in the folds of genetic memory, the panoramas and terrestrial landscapes that persisted with a certain melancholy within him.

This convinced him that his race should leave the Ocean, and that sooner or later the Aquamancers would return to dry land. It was a circle that would be closed.

He had taught Karia that the Risen Lands had been the cradle of civilisation, from where all the animate races had originated, and that that civilisation *had walked*, with its feet firmly on the ground.

Iguain couldn't get the mosaic of his thoughts in order.

As an Aquamancer he knew that the Risen Land Cultures had all ended badly, and that every land-based civilisation was but a fragment in a distributed memory. They, vice-versa, were alive and would remain so until the Sun imploded.

For the Council, the Risen Lands were a fearsome environment, dry, exposed to intense radiation, and above all they offered none of that support provided by water that made moving in the sea so pleasant and less tiring than on land.

It was bizarre that a planet almost completely covered by the Ocean should be called Earth. Sooner or later it would have to be renamed "Aqua".

"I'm going to take the seeds anyway Iguain, with or without your permission. Even though you saved my life, you cannot expect me to sacrifice my people for a question of politics."

Aruna addressed the display with a pleading tone.

"Custodian, I beg you. The seeds must leave this place... I came here to take some samples. Allow my people to be able to plant them again."

"I have awaited a Planter for centuries. Preservation is a means unto planting. You may take two seeds of each type left in the vault."

Aruna was overjoyed, but did not know exactly what to do, nor did she have any idea how to transport the seeds. She was scared of ruining them, of accidentally destroying in an instant her own future.

Then Iguain had a change of heart, turning back with shuffling steps.

"Aruna, I have not told you everything. I did come here for another reason. I want to take us all back to a point when nothing had yet been compromised. I want to put evolution back on the right track."

"What do you mean?"

"I mean that any child born today inherits genes and learns from experience, but she also has the use of words, thoughts, and tools that were invented by others in other places and other eras. The animate beings exist because, on the contrary to other species, they know how to accumulate culture and pass on this information, not only across the Ocean, but also across time, from generation to generation. I think, though, that this progress is cyclic, not linear. The human civilisation was a disaster for the biosphere. The next will be able to value the environment and read its signs.

"So, have you changed your mind?"

"Partially. Karia will return to the Council, whereas I will come with you, if you have nothing against the idea."

Iguain's daughter accepted the decision, perhaps she had already known in her heart that her father would not forgo this opportunity to finally leave the Ocean.

"I'll tell them that I got separated from you. And you dad, you can come back to Saxayé when you have finished."

As she said it, Karia feared that that day would not come any time soon.

From the repaired chronicles of Kilimanjaro

The altitude caused Iguain some days of nausea and spells of dizziness. Born to resist the pressure of the water, his body was vulnerable to the rarefied air. However, when he saw the great size of the Giant Sequoias he forgot any suffering he was going through. These beings were the most incredible creatures he had ever seen.

Aruna introduced him to her family and old Canderum of the Purple Feathers.

In the days that followed, the young woman was frequently away from the Nest, intent on coordinating the teams of planters that had started to work along the slopes of Kilimanjaro.

Returning in the evenings, tired but happy, Aruna told Iguain how in time every Aeromancer would inherit a mixture of seeds, a precious legacy to manage and make "yield". She imagined flights of Aeromancers flying around to pollinate plants and flowers. She imagined spreading the seeds to the other tribes. She imagined descending from the peaks, as the legend foretold.

Iguain, for his part never went too far from the Nest, where the Aeromancers had prepared him a pool for his ablutions. He learned the local customs, he sat on the edge of the Solar Corolla contemplating the marine horizon, which in his mind would pull back and give way to a new unexplored Land, where people could return to walking.

He was not anxious to return to Saxayé, it did not worry him: he had initiated a process of transformation, and even though the consequences of his decision would take a very long time to reach their conclusion, he was at peace with himself.

Canderum glided down next to him. Standing on thin legs, he relied on the support of a stick.

"Look over there... On the left."

The Aeromancer pointed with a finger, and Iguain, focussing, saw what the other was looking at: whole swarms of spores floating in the air.

"Our races will meet again, this time on the shores of the Ocean, Canderum."

"And from there we will go on together."

"As has already happened, but differently."

The two elderly men did not have much else to ask of life, except to observe it continue and recreate itself.

Table of Contents

Designed and typeset by Alda Teodorani
Cover illustration by K. A. Teryna